P9-CMX-092

Pablo and Birdy

ALSO BY ALISON McGHEE

Maybe a Fox

Firefly Hollow

Star Bright

So Many Days

Little Boy

Someday

Pablo and Birdy

ALISON McGHEE

illustrated by ANA JUAN

atheneum

A CAITLYN DLOUHY BOOK

Atheneum Books for Young Readers
New York London Toronto Sydney New Delhi

ATHENEUM BOOKS FOR YOUNG READERS
An imprint of Simon & Schuster Children's Publishing Division
1230 Avenue of the Americas, New York, New York 10020

This book is a work of fiction. Any references to historical events, real people, or real places are used fictitiously. Other names, characters, places, and events are products of the author's imagination, and any resemblance to actual events or places or persons, living or dead, is entirely coincidental.

For information about special discounts for bulk purchases, please contact Simon & Schuster Special Sales at 1-866-506-1949 or business@simonandschuster.com.
The Simon & Schuster Speakers Bureau can bring authors to your live event. For more information or to book an event, contact the Simon & Schuster Speakers Bureau at 1-866-248-3049 or visit our website at www.simonspeakers.com.
Book design by Sonia Chaghatzbanian and Irene Metaxatos
The text for this book was set in Guardi LT Std.
The illustrations for this book were rendered in pencil.
Manufactured in the United States of America
0717 FFG
First Edition
10 9 8 7 6 5 4 3 2 1
Library of Congress Cataloging-in-Publication Data
Names: McGhee, Alison, 1960– author. | Juan, Ana, illustrator.
Title: Pablo and Birdy / Alison McGhee ; illustrated by Ana Juan.
Description: First edition. | New York : Atheneum, 2017. | "A Caitlyn Dlouhy Book." | Summary: Pablo, nearly ten, has many questions about his origins and how he arrived at Isla as a baby, but finding the answers may mean losing his lifetime companion, Birdy the parrot.
Identifiers: LCCN 2016025250 | ISBN 9781481470261 (hardcover : alk. paper) | ISBN 9781481470285 (eBook)
Subjects: | CYAC: Identity—Fiction. | Parrots—Fiction. | Human-animal relationships—Fiction. | Talking birds—Fiction. | Foster parents—Fiction. | Islands—Fiction.
Classification: LCC PZ7.M4784675 Pab 2017 | DDC [Fic]—dc23
LC record available at https://lccn.loc.gov/2016025250

For all those who build new
lives in distant lands
— A. M.

Pablo and Birdy

ONE

READY, BIRDY?" PABLO said, and he held out his finger for her. "Up you go."

Up she jumped. Out the door, careful not to wake Emmanuel, who was asleep behind the closed door of his bedroom, and down the four flights of stairs they went. It was spring, and the town of Isla was quiet at dawn, with the sun just beginning to glimmer on the ocean a few blocks away. But the chickens and pigeons and parrots were already up and about, scratching and clucking around the empty sidewalks.

Soon the shops and cafés would open for business. Soon Pablo and Emmanuel would unlock Seafaring Souvenirs for the day. Pablo would prop open the double doors and wheel the T-shirt racks into the sunshine. Soon the old double-decker red bus would lumber its way down the street, tourists with their sun hats leaning out from the open windows.

But not yet.

Pablo's bike leaned against the side of their apartment building, hidden behind the bougainvillea. Birdy clung to his forearm, her talons gripping his skin, as he wheeled it out. She jumped into the basket that Pablo had bolted to the handlebars, Pablo swung his leg over the frame, and they were off.

Past Pierre's Goodies and Lula Tattoo, past the Parrot Café and Maria's Critter Clinic they went. They took a right at the end of the block, cruised past the Parrot Rescue Sanctuary, through the palm trees, and onto the boardwalk. Pablo leaned the bike against the railing by the wooden stairs that led to the beach and crooked his forearm again for Birdy.

"Up you go."

Once they were down by the water, she fluttered to the top of his head and dug in with her talons.

"Careful now, Birdy-bird," he said. "That's my brain up there, you know."

Birdy swatted him on the ear with her wing. Pablo held his pointer finger straight up in the air and Birdy nipped it gently with her beak. There were many parrots who would take advantage of an unguarded finger, but not Birdy. Not when it came to Pablo, anyway.

"Hold on tight now," he said, and he hopped down onto the sand.

Birdy held on tight. The shoreline was smoothed by the high tide, unmarred by footsteps or paw prints. No one but Pablo and Birdy was out. A lone orange shovel poked up, half-covered with sand, next to a dune. Later today the beach would be busy and noisy with little kids, boogie boarders, fishermen nosing their boats into the marina at the far edge of the harbor, and the coconut man and the *pepitas* woman trudging barefoot down the beach, hawking their wares. But right now, the beach was all theirs.

"Want to fly?" Pablo asked. Birdy jumped down to his shoulder and ducked her head into his neck. That meant yes.

"Hold on tight then," he said, and she dug her talons into his shoulder. He put one hand over them for extra measure. "*Uno, dos, tres . . .*" and down the beach they went. Birdy held on tight, Pablo gradually increased his speed from a jog to a sprint, and then, in a *whoosh*, Birdy spread her wings as wide as they could go. The breeze blew Pablo's hair back, and for a moment he felt as if his feet might leave the ground. Was this what flying felt like? Even a little bit? He wished he knew. But Pablo was a boy, not a bird, so he could only guess.

One thing he knew for sure was that this was as close as Birdy ever came to actual flying, and she loved it. She swayed on his shoulder, her talons clinging tight and her head lifted to the breeze. Almost-flying was Pablo and Birdy's morning ritual. Some people walked their dogs, but Pablo? He flew his bird down the beach. Pablo ran and ran and ran, until he had to stop and catch his breath. They were at the far end of the beach now, no one else around. Only gulls, with their perpetual hunger, wheeled and cried above them, scanning the beach for something to eat. Pablo shaded his eyes and watched them. Birdy's talons clenched and released on his shoulder. Did she wish that she, too, could soar into the sky? It must be hard to be a bird who couldn't fly.

"Birdy?" Pablo spoke softly, so that even if someone had been nearby, only Birdy would hear him. He slid his feet forward so that he was standing right at the shoreline. "Do you remember way back all those years ago? When it was just you and me?"

She dug her talons in a bit, her way of letting him know that she was listening.

"Because I don't," he said.

She shifted her weight from side to side. His fingers found and closed over the necklace he never took off, his *Dios me bendiga* necklace. The stone pendant, with a tiny hole drilled through it, was strung on a narrow leather band. Pablo kept it hidden beneath his T-shirt. Looking out at the water, it was hard to believe that they were at the edge of an ocean. The waves were tiny right now, sloshing in and out like water in a baby's bath-tub, and they tickled his toes.

"Do you remember the big storm that Emmanuel says came through the day before we got here?"

This was the same question he asked her every year. And every year, she was silent. She dug her talons in a little harder. Still listening.

"It's that time of year," Pablo said. "They're going to start in again."

Birdy's talons tightened again. She was the only one he talked to about things like this, and she always let him know she was listening.

"'Double digits!'" Pablo said in a fake grown-up voice. "'What are you going to do for your birthday?'"

Behind them came the soft plop of a coconut, dropping from a palm tree onto the sand. The water wasn't always calm like this. The ocean had a mind of its own. If it were high tide instead of low, the way it was now, Pablo would be standing underwater. And if the winds whipped up the way they sometimes did, the fronds of the palm trees would be blowing in a single direction. Huge waves were known to roar right over the beach and up the stairs and the boardwalk. When a storm was on the way, the inhabitants of Isla got ready. Pierre nailed boards over the big picture window of his bakery. Lula closed and latched the shutters on Lula Tattoo. Maria gathered up all the animals staying at the clinic and took them to her house, sheltered by the pine forest at the other end of town. Emmanuel and Pablo wheeled in the T-shirt racks, rolled up the awnings, buttressed the double doors with sandbags, and locked up tight.

But today there was no storm and no hint of one on the horizon. The breeze that blew today was soft.

"It's not even my real birthday," Pablo muttered. "They should call it my who-knows-what-his-real-birthday-is day. My non-birthday."

The day after a major storm could bring all manner of flotsam floating in on the waves: pieces of driftwood, the smashed hull of a fishing boat, buoys, bottles, skeletons of enormous fish. Once, even though it was hard to believe, a baby had come floating in to shore.

Pablo had been that baby.

TWO

EVERYONE WHO LIVED in Isla knew the story of Birdy and Pablo. After all, Isla was a tiny town, and all the townspeople had been there the day, more than nine years ago now, that the little inflatable swimming pool came floating in on the tide. They had woken to the sound of Emmanuel shouting from the shore. It was dawn and he had been down there on the beach as usual, the way he always was the day after a big storm, waiting for whatever the waves might bring: sea glass or unusual shells or driftwood or some other kind of treasure. Things that he could sell in his souvenir store.

Sometimes he brought a sack to hold the things he collected, but not on that particular day. On that day, Emmanuel's hands were empty.

"At first I thought it was a huge fish," he would say when recounting the story. "A shark or a dolphin, or maybe even a whale."

Emmanuel had stood barefoot at the waterline, his pants rolled up against the waves, and watched the strange object float in. Closer and closer it came, gradually taking shape.

"It happened during the winds of change, if you remember, the morning after that wild storm"—and everyone did remember, because that storm had been particularly wild—"and strange things wash up after wild storms."

Emmanuel had stood still, watching and waiting. It wasn't a fish. Nor was it a boat, or a piece of driftwood, or a tangled mess of seaweed.

"I was prepared for anything," he said.

Anything, that is, except a baby.

When he was sure what his eyes were telling him, he ran straight into the waves.

"Baby!" he shouted. "It's a baby! In a swimming pool! And, and . . . a bird!"

At first no one heard his shouts. The previous night had been filled with furious winds and restless dreams, and most of the townspeople were still asleep. In the first light of the sun, alone, Emmanuel gathered the inflatable pool into his arms. So focused was he on the baby, sound asleep, held securely beneath a latticework of knotted twine, that he barely paid attention to the bird who stood guard, her talons gripped tightly on the twine. In fact, he tried to shoo her off.

But she wasn't about to let go.

Her talons were latched in a death grip on the twine that bound the baby into the swimming pool. In the hurried moment that Emmanuel looked at the bird, tearing his attention away from the sleeping dark-haired baby, he registered her as worn out, with dull eyes and limp, dirty feathers. Scrawny. Severely stressed. But there was something beautiful about her nonetheless.

"I could see it even in that first moment," he would tell his friends later. "She was special. There was a . . . a magnificence about her."

Emmanuel was right. It wasn't until weeks later, when the bird refused to leave the baby's side, that everyone else saw how unusual she was. No one had seen a parrot with her coloring before. Lavender, with under-feathers of iridescent blue-green. She anticipated the baby's needs, bringing him bits of chopped up mango or banana when he was hungry. Pulling his little green blanket up over his chest when he fell asleep.

"She must have been with Pablo from the beginning," Emmanuel said. "She was like a bird mother, watching over him. It was only when she was sure that I meant him no harm that she let go of the twine."

Emmanuel had carried the baby, still sleeping, still secured in the inflatable pool, back to his souvenir store at the end of the block. The bird jumped to his shoulder and dug her talons in tight. Every now and then she leaned forward and nipped Emmanuel's ear, as if to show him who was boss.

"I tried talking to her," Emmanuel said. "She's a parrot, after all. But she didn't want to listen. *She* was the one in charge. Not me."

At this point in the story, he raised his arms like wings and fixed his listeners with a fierce stare, imitating the way Birdy had stood guard in front of baby Pablo.

"I told her not to worry, that the baby was safe now. And eventually she believed me, but it took weeks."

Early risers who were just opening their windows or doors to let in the morning breeze had stopped in amazement at the sight of their friend Emmanuel and his bundle.

"It's a baby," Emmanuel kept saying, as if somehow that would explain everything.

By the time he got to the store, the bird was

drooping with exhaustion. Lula was sweeping the sidewalk in front of her henna tattoo shop. Pierre had just propped open the door to Pierre's Goodies.

"You should have seen the looks on your faces," Emmanuel always said when recounting the story. "I thought nothing could make either of you speechless, but you were speechless that day."

"You can't deny it was a wondrous sight," Pierre always said at this point. "There you were, Pablo"—he would nod at Pablo as if his arrival had happened just recently—"wrapped and knotted into that little swimming pool with so much twine that it's a wonder you could breathe. *Mon dieu!* But you just slept on."

Lula would look at Birdy and shake her head, as if she still couldn't believe that Birdy existed. "And there you were, Birdy, holding on to Pablo for dear life."

"For dear life," Pierre would echo, and Emmanuel would nod.

Birdy, silent as always, closed her eyes and cocked her head whenever she heard those words, *for dear life*, as if they reminded her of something. But what that something was, no one knew.

THREE

PABLO WASN'T A baby anymore. He was turning ten in a couple of weeks, at least according to Emmanuel, who had decided to celebrate Pablo's birthday every year on the anniversary of the day he had floated in on the waves. Every year at this time he had a hard time sleeping. He didn't remember anything about his arrival in Isla. It was a mystery. Where had he come from? How had he ended up out on the ocean alone, with only Birdy to watch over him? These questions were always with him, but he only let himself think—*really* think—about them once a year. And now was the once.

"I wish you could give me a clue," he said. "Anything."

The beach in early morning was where they came when Pablo needed to talk about things he couldn't tell anyone but Birdy. They were still the only ones here, but that wouldn't last long. Already Pablo could hear the faint purr of a fishing boat motor in the direction of the marina.

"All the other birds talk," he reminded Birdy.

First Emmanuel, and then Pablo, when he grew older, had tried to get Birdy to talk. She was a parrot, after all, and most parrots could be taught to speak. Birdy's origins were a mystery, but maybe, if she remembered and could speak even a few words or phrases, they could figure out something of her past. Emmanuel had tried to teach her a few words—*Mi nombre es Birdy*, for example—but she remained silent. Sometimes even now, when they were alone on the beach, Pablo would coax her to say something. Nothing silly like *Polly want a cracker?* which was a tourist thing to say, but *Let's fly, Pablo*, or its Spanish equivalent, *Vamos a volar, Pablo*. But even when he tempted her with treats, especially diced pineapple, she never made a sound except when she was deeply asleep. And that was more like a mutter, or a sigh, instead of actual words.

"Yes, they all talk," he said again, "even if they don't have a lot to say."

"Hey!" came a nearby squawk. "Watch what you're saying!"

Oh no. The Committee was already up and after them. Pablo turned, Birdy still on his shoulder, in the direction of the squawk. There was Peaches, the squawker, fluttering across the boardwalk. Mr. Chuckles was right behind her, followed by Sugar Baby and Rhody. Peaches was an African gray, Mr. Chuckles was a budgie, and Sugar Baby was a monk parakeet.

Rhody was not a parrot at all—he was a Rhode Island Red rooster—but he seemed to think he was. He disdained the other Isla chickens, who clucked and strutted their way along the side-walks and in the cafés, in favor of hanging out with the parrots.

These four birds roamed the town together like a roving band of greeters, which was why Pablo had nicknamed them the Committee. Down the boardwalk and across the sand they came, hopping and fluttering and clucking. Birdy dug her talons into Pablo and hung on tight. She held herself a little apart from the others, as always. Silent, as always.

"What day is it?" said Sugar Baby.

"A day of questions that I don't know the answers to," Pablo said. "That's what day it is. Which is why I came down here to talk to Birdy alone, without you all eavesdropping."

"Hey! Watch what you're saying!" squawked Peaches.

"*You* watch what you're saying, Peaches."

"HAHAHAHAHA!" This from Mr. Chuckles, who enjoyed a good laugh even when there was nothing to laugh at. Now he cocked his head at

Birdy and fluffed up his feathers. "Nice threads!" he said. "Lookin' sharp!"

Birdy didn't even glance at him. This was typical, but Mr. Chuckles had never stopped trying to get a reaction out of her. Sometimes Pablo thought he had a crush on Birdy.

"HAHAHAHAHA!" Mr. Chuckles said now, as if to cover up his embarrassment that Birdy was ignoring him. "HAHAHAHAHA!"

"Enough now," said Pablo. "Time to get back."

He had come here with Birdy for the express purpose of talking to her about his birthday, which Emmanuel and everyone else looked forward to every year but which Pablo dreaded. But it was no use trying to talk now, not with the Committee eavesdropping.

"What day is it?" sighed Sugar Baby again.

Sugar Baby was a quiet little parakeet who wasn't fond of the beach. She liked to stay in close range of Lula and Lula's tattoo shop. Each member of the Committee had a special human, one preferred above others. Lula was Sugar Baby's favorite human in the same way that Mr. Chuckles preferred Pierre, Rhody liked the flower lady, and Peaches was a fan of Emmanuel. And of course, they all loved Maria, the veterinarian. All creatures, whether birds or dogs or cats or ferrets or alpacas, loved Maria.

None of the Committee members was like Birdy, though. No bird in the world was devoted to another human the way Birdy was devoted to Pablo.

FOUR

ISLA WAS FAMOUS for its birds. They strutted in and out of the shops and cafés, roosted in bushes and trees, and raised their young without fear of humans. They were fed and sheltered and photographed and celebrated. Birds were one of the main tourist attractions of the town.

Even when they misbehaved, they were tolerated. Take Mr. Chuckles on Sunday mornings, for example. He was a self-appointed fashion judge, and Sunday was his favorite day of the week. Every Sunday morning he installed himself, along with the Committee, in the lower limb of the box elder tree just outside the church.

"Nice threads!"

"Hmm."

"HAHAHAHAHA!"

Nice threads! was what everyone wanted to hear. No one wanted a *Hmm,* but even *hmms* were preferred over a Mr. Chuckles *HAHAHA-HAHA*. Over time, the churchgoers had gradually stepped up their attire. It was to the point now where women tried to outdo one another with their hats and men with their colorful shirts.

"Mr. Chuckles is a tough judge," Lula said.

"His standards are high," Pierre said.

"I'm glad I don't go to church," Emmanuel said. "That's all I have to say."

Yes, Isla was famous for its birds, especially its talking birds. All the talkers in the town were familiar species: African gray parrots, mynah birds, Amazons, cockatiels, conures, monk parakeets, macaws.

But Isla was also famous for something else,

something that had never been proven. For many years rumors had persisted that Isla might once have been home to, or perhaps a stopping point for, a certain kind of bird whose existence had never been verified.

The name of this bird was the Seafaring Parrot, which also went by the nickname of Seafarer. Legend had it that Seafaring Parrots possessed special abilities known to no other parrot, or any other bird, for that matter. They lived on the ocean and spent nearly all their time on the wing, soaring high above the waves on the strong ocean winds. Reported sightings of Seafarers were very rare, and only when the winds of change were blowing: straight onshore or straight offshore, which happened only once every ten years or so. There was an old fisherman's saying, familiar to every islander: *The winds of change mean fortune lost or fortune gained.*

But the most unusual trait of the Seafaring Parrots, according to legend, had to do with sound. Sound exists in vibrations. As those vibrations grow slower and slower, the frequency becomes inaudible to nearly all creatures. Humans, with their unexceptional ears, could hear a sound at the moment it was made, and thereafter only in memory. But not the remarkable ears of a Seafaring Parrot. For them, all sound lived on for all eternity. Their ears were so finely tuned that supposedly, at any given moment in time, a Seafarer could hear and reproduce all the sounds ever made:

The laughter of everyone who ever lived.

The cries of everyone who ever lived.

The scuffle of feet and paws, human and animal. The sigh of a summer breeze, the freight-train howl of an oncoming tornado. The lapping of waves at the southern shore, the groan of an iceberg calving in the Arctic Ocean. The shriek of pain from a child who'd stubbed his toe. The sigh of a mother at the first sight of her newborn baby. The angry shouts of a couple in the heat of an argument. The song of a father singing his child to sleep.

Pablo had tried to comprehend the hugeness of this.

"*Every* sound?" he had said, the night long ago when Emmanuel first explained the legend of the Seafarer.

"Every sound."

"In the entire *world*?"

Emmanuel nodded. "Every single sound, every single voice. They can bring them all back. According to the legend, anyway."

Tonight they were sitting in the kitchen, playing cards again and talking about Seafarers. Cards and conversation was their routine. Emmanuel would put the Buena Vista Social Club on his old record player and Pablo would make his famous cheese quesadillas, which was what Emmanuel called them even though they were famous only between the two of them. They would play rummy while Birdy hopped back and forth from one to the other, pushing her beak at the cards she wanted them to play or discard.

It was Pablo's turn to draw, but he was

distracted. The legend was fascinating, and it always made him wonder about something. Birdy was a parrot, but no one—not even Dr. Maria, who would certainly know, because she was a veterinarian—could say for sure what kind of parrot she was. Was it possible, even remotely possible, that Birdy was a Seafarer? Pablo and Birdy had washed up onshore during the winds of change, after all.

But wait. Seafarers were capable of flying tremendous distances. And no one had ever seen Birdy fly. The most she could manage was that awkward flutter of hers, from the bike basket to his forearm, say, or from his forearm to his shoulder. And what about sound? Seafarers could reproduce every sound that had ever existed, and Birdy was the quietest bird in all of Isla. No, Birdy couldn't be a Seafarer. Which was fine with Pablo, because he loved her just the way she was.

Sometimes, between rounds of rummy, Pablo would airplane Birdy around the kitchen and living room. She would grip his forearm tight and he would sail her through the air, around and around. It was the evening, indoor version of their almost-flying on the beach.

"No one knows if the legend's true, of course," Emmanuel said, putting down his cards. "I've been hearing about Seafarers my whole life, and I'm a grown man who's never seen one. People have claimed to see them out at sea, but who knows if they're real or not."

"But the part about sound vibrations is real?"

Emmanuel nodded, as if Pablo had asked an excellent question. "Some say sound never entirely disappears. It just vibrates at lower and lower frequencies, so that our poor ears can't hear it even the moment after it happens."

That was usually where conversation about Seafarers stopped, with a sad look on Emmanuel's face at how inferior human ears were to Seafarer ears. But tonight Pablo kept going.

"If the legend *is* true," he said, "and somewhere out there is a bird who can still hear the voices of everyone who ever lived, that means she could even hear . . ."

"Everything," Emmanuel said, finishing Pablo's sentence for him. "Yes, *mi Pablito,* everything."

That hadn't been what Pablo was going to say, though. Pablo was thinking about his original family, whoever they might have been. Maybe he had once had a father. Brothers and sisters. A mother. Was it possible that he, Pablo, had once had a mother? But Emmanuel never brought it up, so Pablo didn't either. He didn't like the thought of hurting Emmanuel's feelings, after all, because Emmanuel had always been a father to him. So he confided only in Birdy.

Sometimes he wished he had never heard the legend of the Seafaring Parrot. It made his head hurt to think about.

FIVE

EMMANUEL WASN'T THE only one who liked to speculate about the Seafaring Parrot. The existence of the bird had long been debated, both in Isla and far beyond its borders. There were those who said the Seafaring Parrot, like the dodo, had once existed but was now extinct. There were those who said that the Seafaring Parrot had never existed. Then there were those who insisted that yes, the Seafaring Parrot did exist, had always existed, and was just extremely rare and extremely reclusive.

Reported sightings of Seafarers usually came in from offshore fishermen. In fact, there had been several such sightings the day before Pablo and Birdy washed up to shore. Those sightings had been reported by television's most zealous Seafaring Parrot reporter, Elmira Toledo, who always wore a trench coat and purple glasses. Elmira had for years made Seafarer sightings her pet project. But no one had been able to follow up the ocean sightings.

Even in school, which was a haphazard sort of affair on Isla, given that there weren't many island children and most learned at the side of their parents, the Seafaring Parrot was the subject of reports and plays and songs. Every year, in fact, the schoolchildren went on a two-week marine expedition in search of the elusive Seafarer. That was the excuse, anyway. If pressed, everyone admitted that they just liked being out on the sea, fishing and diving and practicing their sailing skills.

Everyone but Pablo, that is, who was deeply

afraid of storms. Besides, no animals, including birds, were allowed onboard, and what good was that? The yearly expedition had set sail a few days ago, but he had stayed behind with Birdy.

"One of us should be here to search from shore," he had told his friend Oswaldo, who agreed.

A major complicating factor when it came to the Seafaring Parrot was that no one was exactly sure what they were supposed to look like. There were no photographs, and eyewitness accounts varied. That didn't stop anyone from having an opinion, however.

"Seafaring Parrots look like African grays," claimed the flower lady. "My grandmother swore to it. Which makes sense, because no other parrot has the talking capabilities of the African gray."

It was true that African grays were renowned for their ability to mimic human voices. Take Peaches, for example. A single "Hey! Watch what you're saying!" could make anyone snap to attention.

"No, no," said the coconut man, who walked the beach lopping the tops off coconuts with his machete, sticking straws into them, and selling them to beachgoers. "When it comes to looks, Seafaring Parrots are a close cousin to the macaw. Everyone knows that."

"Everyone does *not* know that," said Maria. "In fact, legend does not specify what the Seafaring Parrot is supposed to look like, other than a parrot."

Maria was descended from a long line of island veterinarians. Her mother and her grandmother and her great-grandmother had all, at some point, presided over the Critter Clinic. Maria always told the truth as she saw it, which was one of the reasons why Pablo sometimes went to the clinic to talk to her. She would give him the straight scoop.

Today was one of those days.

"Scram, Committee," he said. "Birdy and I have an appointment with Dr. Maria."

This wasn't strictly true, but Maria and Pablo

had an unspoken agreement that he was welcome in the clinic anytime. The Committee clustered around him. They didn't like to be left out of anything.

"Hey! Watch what you're saying!"

"Nice threads!"

"Cock-a-doodle-doo!"

"What day is it?" Sugar Baby said, in her small voice.

"It's a day when I want to see Maria without you all eavesdropping," said Pablo. "That's what day it is. You're always butting in on other people's business. Now go bug someone else."

The Committee grumbled off down the street. Maria was in the clinic alone, which meant that Pablo wouldn't have to wait until she was finished examining an alpaca this time. The alpaca owner was something of a hypochondriac, who brought one or more of his three alpacas into the clinic at least once a week.

"Pablo," Maria said. "Birdy."

Maria greeted both humans and animals the

same way, which was another thing Pablo liked about her. He also appreciated that she kept their conversations private. She called it "doctor-critter confidentiality," and even though Pablo wasn't a critter and Maria wasn't his doctor, it was close enough.

"Maria, have you decided what kind of parrot you think Birdy is?"

He had been asking Maria this question for years now, but each time he asked, she considered it carefully. He set Birdy on Maria's desk, where she stood, shifting from one foot to the other. Then she ducked her head into her feathers. Maria might not be sick of the question, but it seemed as if Birdy was.

"Well," said Maria, "I've never seen a parrot with her kind of lavender coloring. It's very unusual. My best guess remains the same, which is that Birdy is a parrot, but an unfamiliar one, not native to Isla."

Maria held out her arm, crooked at the elbow, as if she were inviting Birdy to do-si-do with her. Birdy untucked her head from her feathers, met the doctor's brown eyes with her own, and jumped up to her arm. It was hard to resist Maria.

"She doesn't talk, though," said Pablo.

"Not all parrots talk."

"She doesn't fly, either."

"She *has* flown, though. She's traveled far. Her wings and feathers tell the story of long, hard voyages by air."

At that, Birdy bent nearly in half and tucked her head into her feathers as far as she could. Maria stroked her feathers with a light but firm touch.

"Sometimes a seabird will be caught up in a strong current and fly halfway around the world," she said. "It's been known to happen."

"Maria, can I ask you another question?" Pablo said.

"You may, Pablo."

Pablo looked around the waiting room, to make sure they were alone and that the alpacas and their anxious owner hadn't shown up unexpectedly.

"Do you think it's possible," he whispered, "that Birdy could be a Seafaring Parrot?"

This was a question he had never asked outright, fearing that Maria would just roll her eyes and tell him that legends were legends, not facts, and that she was a woman of science. He'd seen her do that more than once, when townspeople got going on the legend of the Seafaring Parrot. But he was almost ten now, and this question had been on his mind for a while. Maria didn't laugh or roll her eyes, thank goodness. She sat down on the chair next to his and regarded him thoughtfully.

"If the legend of the Seafaring Parrot is true," she said, "then Seafarers can't live without flight. Flying is in their souls. A Seafarer who can't fly would be like a fisherman without the sea."

This was something that Pablo could understand. Isla, nestled just off the southern shore of the US, was a town of fisherfolk and boats and sea, the sea with its salt water and its waves, curling and unfurling on the sand.

"No one's ever seen Birdy fly, have they?" the doctor said now. "And she seems to have survived so far."

They both looked at Birdy, who was most definitely alive. So it must be as Maria said: that Birdy was an unfamiliar kind of non-talking parrot. No one knew more about parrots than Maria, after all, just like her mother and grandmother and great-grandmother before her.

"She loves it when I almost-fly her down the beach, though. I wish—" but Pablo stopped midsentence. Birdy was slowly, ever so slowly, lifting her wings to their full extent. She looked from Pablo to the doctor, and she jumped down from Maria's arm and took a step forward, and then another and another, until she was at the very edge of the desk. As if she were about to step right off it into thin air.

"Birdy," said the doctor, "what are you doing?" and she and Pablo leaned forward to catch her in case she fell. The three of them stayed frozen for a minute, until Birdy—with what sounded almost like a sigh—lowered her wings and ducked her head. The doctor placed a hand on her talons, as if to reassure her.

"That was strange," she said. "Birdy hasn't been plucking out any of her feathers lately, has she?"

"No."

"Because that would be a sign of distress. A sign that something needed to change."

"Like what?"

"I don't know," Maria said. "Look, Pablo. Seafaring Parrots are supposed to be magical birds. But their endless flying, and their ability to reproduce every sound ever made, is what makes them magic. And in all the time she's lived here, Birdy has never flown, has she?"

"No."

"Nor has she talked. Has she?"

"No," Pablo said. "The only noise she makes, once in a while, is when she's asleep."

"Anything understandable?"

"No. It's more like a whisper."

The doctor slowly, with just one finger, stroked Birdy's feathers from neck to end of wing. Over and over she drew her finger down the length of Birdy's wings, first one wing and then the other, as if she could mend by touch alone whatever invisible thing was broken.

SIX

THAT NIGHT SOMETHING changed.

Pablo was used to the sound of Birdy's sleeping sigh. When it happened, she was always sound asleep next to his hammock on the upended old suitcase that had come with Emmanuel when he left Cuba as a little boy with his family. Birdy slept on it with one foot pulled up into her feathers. Was she dreaming? Maybe, because she would twitch and sometimes shudder.

Birdy's sigh was more of a whisper than anything else, but it sounded like a woman's whisper. And not Maria or Lula or the flower lady or anyone else that Pablo knew. If many months went by without a sound, Pablo wondered if he himself had dreamed it up—if his memories of Birdy's sleeping sigh were something that happened only in his own mind.

But that night, when the moon was high and round and making a flickering path on the sea beyond the window, he startled awake to the sound of an actual voice, a woman's voice.

"Pablo. Pobrecito Pablo."

Pablo. Poor little Pablo.

Pablo lifted his head from the pillow and half sat up in the hammock. "Birdy? Did you just say something?"

But there was no answer. She was sound asleep. Pablo lay awake for a while, then decided that he must have been dreaming. If Birdy could talk, she would surely have done so before now. Look at all the times he had tried to teach her to say even a single word, but she had never tried to mimic a human voice. Unlike the other parrots.

Visitors to Isla loved the parrots who roamed the streets and called down from the trees they hung out in. And the parrots, especially the Committee, liked that kind of attention. Why else were they usually found at the double-decker bus stop? Loud Mr. Chuckles and squawky Peaches liked to perch directly on the bus stop sign and startle the tourists as they got off.

"HAHAHAHAHA!"

"Hey! Watch what you're saying!"

Sugar Baby would follow up in her soft voice. "What day is it?" she would sigh. "What day is it?"

Sugar Baby melted hearts with that question. She was small and adorable and more successful at getting treats from diners at the Parrot Café than either Mr. Chuckles or Peaches, which annoyed them both. Peaches had taken to hanging upside down from the strings of little white lights—as an African gray, she had that ability—just for the attention it got her. And Mr. Chuckles's laugh was infectious. Both of them did well enough for themselves in terms of treats

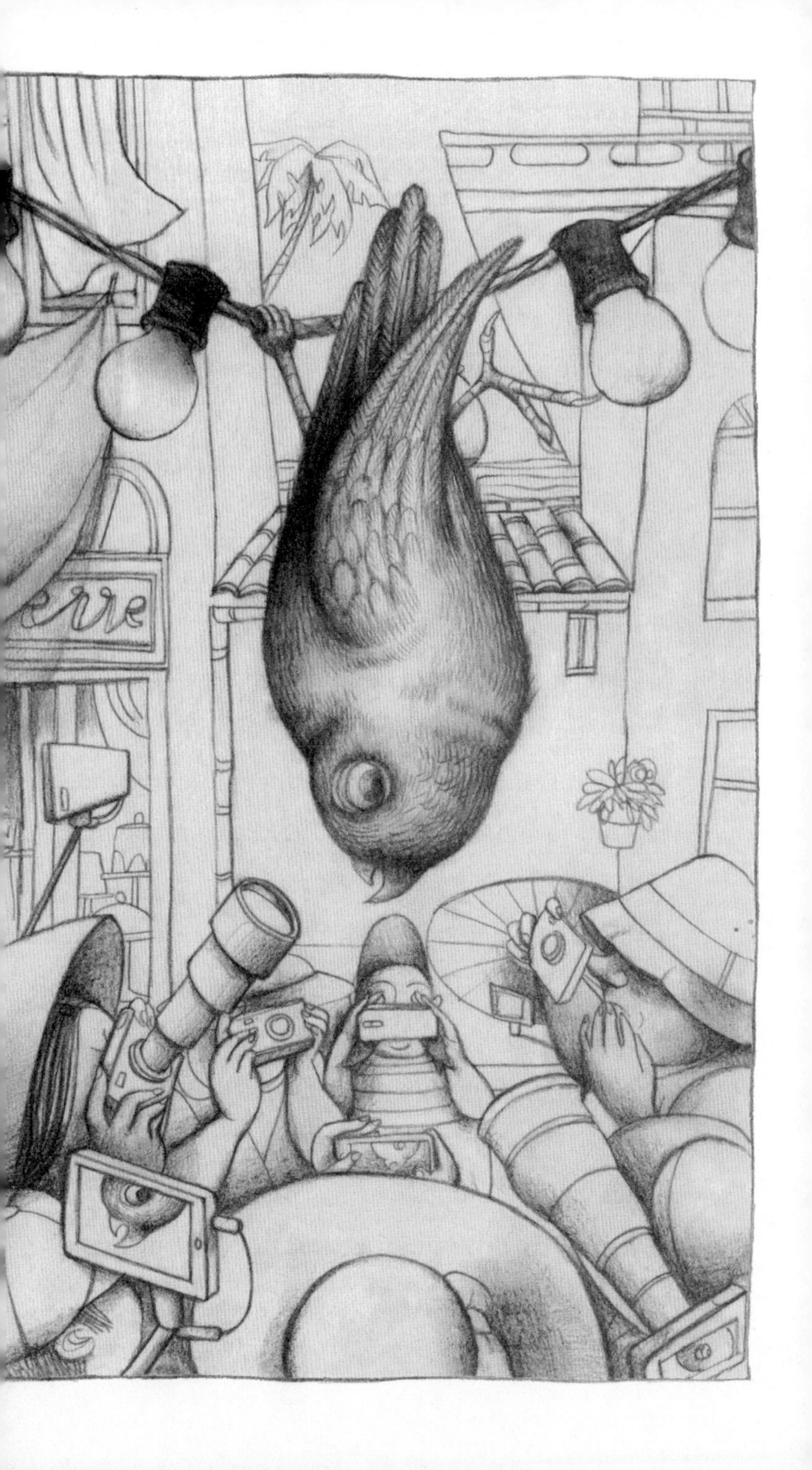

and attention, if not as well as Sugar Baby.

Rhody, poor Rhody, who could only cluck and scratch and crow but still persisted in thinking of himself as a parrot, had long ago had to resort to snatching lettuce leaves and ears of corn right off the plates.

Emmanuel was of the opinion that Birdy did talk, in a way.

"Maybe not in words," he said. "But that bird knows how to get her point across."

He was referring to the Birdy swat, which everyone in Isla was familiar with. When Birdy felt that someone wasn't treating Pablo right, or if, God forbid, she felt that Pablo was in danger, she would leap to her feet, raise her wing, and swat whoever was at fault. Pablo had never felt her wrath, but then again, he was her beloved.

Emmanuel also believed that Birdy, even if she didn't talk herself, understood at least some speech. One night, when they were playing rummy and listening to the Buena Vista Social Club, Birdy fluttering between the two of them and peering at their cards, Emmanuel had told Pablo a secret.

"This happened when you first arrived," he said. "You had no clothes, no belongings, no papers, nothing but your necklace and that green blanket. You had no name, or so I thought anyway, and I was trying to think of a good one. You lay in the dresser drawer—that was what I used as a crib—looking up at me with those serious dark eyes, and I started trying out possibilities."

Emmanuel had started going through names, one after another: José. Diego. Tomás. Juan. Gabriel. Jesús. Samuel. None of them had seemed right to him.

"Those all sound like good names," Pablo said.

"They were, but none of them felt like the perfect fit," said Emmanuel. "So I kept going. Felipe. Rodrigo. Bautista. No, no, no. Then came Pablo, and that was when Birdy leaped to the rim of the dresser drawer and balanced there. She raised both wings"—he raised his arms in imitation—"and stood staring at me. And that was it," he said. "Pablo it was."

And Pablo it had remained.

"I believe she was telling me, in her own way, that Pablo was your given name," Emmanuel said. "I believe that was Birdy's way of talking to me."

If that was her way of talking, Birdy wasn't at all like the other parrots in town. She wasn't a budgie or a monk parakeet or a blue-fronted Amazon or a conure or a macaw or any of the talking birds that lived in Isla.

"What about Birdy?" Pablo asked. "How'd she get her name?"

"From you."

"*Me?* How?"

"One morning, a few days after you arrived, I woke up to hear you laughing. I looked over at the dresser drawer and there was Birdy, doing a little dance on the side of it." Emmanuel smiled. "She was dancing, and you were laughing, and then you waved your hands and said 'Birdy.'"

He began to shuffle the cards. "Birdy was your very first word, *mi Pablito*."

"Well, it *is* a good word," Pablo said.

Birdy, who had been silently watching them the whole time, ducked her head into Pablo's shoulder. She seemed to agree.

SEVEN

DESPITE THE LACK of an actual Seafarer, the shopkeepers who lived in Isla made the most of its reputation as the place where one would most likely be spotted. There was the Parrot Café, there were T-shirts featuring the favorite phrases of the chattiest town parrots, there were glass-bottom boat tours of the "Famous Seafarer Spotting Grounds." Lula designed a new parrot henna tattoo each week. Pierre's parrot-shaped cookies with neon frosting were nearly as popular as his perennial bestseller elephant ears. Isla Ice Cream even featured Parrot Sorbet, which Pablo secretly thought was a terrible name for rainbow sherbet but which sold by the bucketful.

As Emmanuel said, "We have to make a living, right? Might as well give the people what they want."

So they did.

Pablo and Emmanuel sold parrot souvenirs of all kinds at Seafaring Souvenirs: mugs with parrots painted on them, maps of Historical Seafaring Parrot possible sightings, cans of Air Possibly Breathed by Seafaring Parrots, coconut candies with wrappers that featured parrots, key chains that featured a parrot with giant talons and a terrifying glare in its eyes. (The key chains were not big sellers.) Emmanuel spent many late nights listening to the Buena Vista Social Club and designing new Seafaring Parrot T-shirts. He was the best T-shirt designer in town, just as Lula was the best tattoo artist.

Pablo himself had a specialty as well: parrot seashell paintings. He collected pretty shells at low tide, then biked them back home, with Birdy perched uncomfortably in the basket on top of the lumpy shells. At night, when the store was closed, he and Emmanuel sat at the table. Emmanuel worked on his T-shirt designs and Pablo, using a miniature sable brush, painted tiny acrylic parrots on the insides of the seashells. Each had a caption: *African Gray*, *Monk Parakeet*, *Budgie*.

Peaches.

Sugar Baby.

Mr. Chuckles.

They were his models, even if they didn't know it. Pablo had even begun painting a tiny Rhody, with the caption *Chicken*, so as not to mislead anyone that Rhody was anything but a parrot wannabe. Tourists were very fond of Pablo's Painted Parrots, which he sold for the reasonable price of one dollar apiece.

From the start, Lula and Pierre had advised Pablo to branch out into painted Seafarers. Tourists had a never-ending hunger for Seafaring

Parrot souvenirs, so why not? "Just make up what one looks like," Lula had said. "Call it an artist's rendering." But Pablo had always refused. He didn't want to paint a parrot with no real-life model to draw from, a parrot that could well be imaginary. Wouldn't that be a lie?

"It would be an embellishment," said Lula.

But an embellishment was a kind of lie too. No. Pablo stuck to the parrots he knew, punctuated by the occasional Rhode Island Red chicken.

In the morning, before the store opened, Pablo and Emmanuel and Lula and Maria usually met at Pierre's Goodies, just down the block from Pablo and Emmanuel's apartment.

"Fortification," Lula referred to their morning get-togethers. "Preparation for the onslaught."

That was life in Isla, where most of the townspeople worked in the tourist trade. Every morning, before they opened their shops for the day, the Isla shopkeepers wandered into Pierre's bakery empty-handed and emerged with lidded cups of coffee or tea and white waxed paper bags. The big Pierre's Goodies picture window displayed an array of pastries: croissants both plain and chocolate; cinnamon, blueberry, and cream scones; and assorted rolls and breads. Parrot cookies with enormous beaks and gumdrop eyes. And of course, Pierre's famous elephant ears.

The Committee liked to peer in the picture window too, even though they were too short to view the pastries unless they fluttered up into the air, which they took turns doing.

"What day is it?"

"Hey! Watch what you're saying!"

"Cock-a-doodle-doo!"

Sometimes they landed on one another, which didn't go over well with any of them.

This morning Pablo and Birdy were the first ones at the bakery. The Committee caught sight of them and began trundling down the sidewalk from the bus stop, Rhody crowing maniacally to get their attention.

Lula was sweeping the sidewalk in front of

her henna tattoo store. Lula was as meticulous about her sweeping as she was about her tattoos. Nearly all of them featured Lula's "artist's renderings" of Seafaring Parrots, with a few seashells and palm trees thrown in. Lula's tattoos were highly sought-after, partly because henna tattoos didn't involve needles, which meant that they didn't hurt, and partly because they faded away in a week or so, which was good because Lula was not a believer in permanent tattoos.

"Give it up, Rhody," she said now. "When will you learn that you're not a parrot and you never will be?"

Rhody crowed again, even louder. The rest of the Committee clustered around Pablo and Birdy, with Peaches nudging Mr. Chuckles to get closer to Pablo. Inside the bakery, Pierre looked up from behind the counter and motioned them in.

"*Bonjour*, Pablo. *Bonjour*, Birdy. Committee"—he waved his arms, shooing the other birds back—"not today. Too crowded."

Pierre was not French, but he had once spent three weeks in Paris, learning the fine points of pastry making, and France had rubbed off on him. His real name was Peter McGarry, but after Paris he had changed the Peter to Pierre and left off the McGarry entirely. He liked to buy a single flower from the flower lady every day, to put in his apron pocket. Today's was a daisy.

"*Pour Mademoiselle Birdy*," he said, and he held out a bowl of diced apple to Pablo. "And for you, *monsieur*." He handed him a cupcake with sprinkles on top in the shape of a birthday candle. There was a small commotion at the door, an abbreviated rooster's crow followed by a squawk. The Committee was doing their best to gain entry. Pierre raised both arms in the air and made as if to charge the door, and once again they retreated to the sidewalk.

"Persistent," Pierre said, "persistent, but Pierre shall triumph." He winked. "Almost your birthday, Pablo, *non*?"

Pablo nodded.

"Double digits?"

"Yeah."

"Any special plans?"

Pablo shook his head.

"I have a special plan," said Lula, who had come in for her morning mint tea and was right behind Pablo. "My special plan is to create a new tattoo in honor of your birthday."

"That's always your special plan," said Pierre. "Every year, another special tattoo."

"Same as you," said Lula. "Another year, another cake."

"I wish you'd both stop," said Pablo.

Oops. He hadn't expected to say that. It had just popped right out of his mouth. That was the kind of thing he would think inside his head, or tell Birdy when they were alone at the shore. It was *not* the kind of thing he ever said to anyone else.

Lula and Pierre looked surprised, and Lula opened her mouth to say something, but the double-decker bus had just pulled up to the curb and a gaggle of tourists came pushing their way in, exclaiming over the elephant ears that Pierre's Goodies was famous for, and Pierre glanced at Pablo and Lula apologetically and got back to work.

Out on the sidewalk again, Pablo set the bowl of diced apple beside him on the bench. The Committee stood by watchfully, hoping that Birdy would feel like sharing, but she ignored them. Lula disappeared into her tattoo shop.

Maria came out of Pierre's carrying a cinnamon roll in one hand and a cup of coffee in the other and sat down on the bench next to Pablo. Across the street, the Critter Clinic was still closed, but a line was beginning to form. A woman sat on the clinic bench with a cat on her lap. A man holding a shoe box, with what looked like a ferret poking its head out of it, sat next to her. A small girl with a teddy bear in her arms stood next to the bench. Stuffed animals were as welcome as living animals at Maria's clinic. She was an equal-opportunity veterinarian.

Now she eyed the small line of patients and their keepers with a practiced eye. They could all wait, apparently, because she took a bite of cinnamon roll and offered it to Pablo.

"No, thank you."

"So," she said. "Almost ten, huh?"

"Yes."

"And do you have any plans?"

"Yes," Pablo said. "I do."

"Care to share?"

"I plan to do something brave."

Yikes! Pablo hadn't expected to say that, either. He didn't even know what the something brave might be. But Maria just sat there, nodding, as if she weren't surprised. Did she think he was the kind of person who did brave things? *Because I'm not,* thought Pablo.

She seemed to be gathering her thoughts to say something. But then a woman with a miniature goat on a leash joined the line at the clinic across the street, the ferret popped right out of the box on the man's lap, and the cat squalled and began swiping at it with its claws. The Committee watched with interest.

"Simmer down there!" squawked Peaches. "Simmer down!"

Maria sighed and got up. She brushed the crumbs off her doctor coat, drank down the rest of her coffee, and looked at Pablo. He braced himself for more questions. About his double-digit birthday, about whatever it was that he had in mind for it. But she just smiled.

"So," she said. "Something brave, huh? I'll be interested to see what that turns out to be."

EIGHT

PABLO AND BIRDY didn't know it, and neither did Maria or Lula or Pierre, but as they were gathering themselves for the tourist onslaught, a young dog, new to Isla, was only a few yards away from them. He was a scruffy little thing who stuck to the shadows. He sidled along the alley that ran behind the buildings on the block, sniffing all the unfamiliar smells of the town. His tail had been broken at some point and hadn't healed properly, so the tip bent to the side and kept brushing against the back of the brick-and-frame buildings that lined the alley.

The dog didn't want to be discovered. This wasn't hard, because the alley was dark and too narrow for cars and bikes. It wasn't the sort of place that pedestrians ventured down either. Lidded garbage cans stood next to the closed back doors of silent stores.

The dog stopped by one of those garbage cans and snuffed around it. This can was particularly delicious smelling. Meat scraps. Carrot peelings. Cake and pie crumbs. Possibly a bone or two, maybe even three.

His stomach growled. His tongue lolled out and he drooled.

It had been a long, long time since the dog had had any food. Three days, or four, or even longer, and the last thing he had eaten was a half-rotten fish, too rotted even for bait, that had washed up onshore. Cast off from a fishing boat, maybe. Stinky though it was, the dog had gobbled it down and then disappeared back into the scrubby woods that lined the shore.

Finally, in the middle of the last night, his hunger had gotten the best of him, and he had slunk into the town itself, drawn to this particular alley because it backed onto the Parrot Café and Pierre's Goodies. Now that the sun was up, he was exploring. So far he hadn't been able to dislodge any garbage can lids, nor were there any discarded scraps of food from pedestrians, not back here.

He moved on and his bent tail brushed against another garbage can. This one smelled of ink and graphite and paper. Nothing edible. Nothing interesting. Onward.

But the farther he crept, the more smells reached his nose. The smells of fresh food. Delicious food. Food of all kinds. He crept on down the alley, following his nose. At the far end was sunlight and color and the sounds of cars and people and maybe even other animals. Birds, certainly. And food. The smell of food, wonderful food, precious food. So much food.

Could he manage to get hold of some of it?

NINE

EVERY YEAR, ON Pablo's non-birthday, Pierre baked him a special cake, Lula designed a new birthday tattoo, and Emmanuel came up with a new theory to explain Pablo's miraculous arrival on the shores of Isla. These celebrations had been going on for almost ten years now. Pablo wished everyone would just quit, but then again, he had never told them that the very idea of his birthday made him sad. And now so much time had gone by that he didn't know how to bring it up, not even with Emmanuel. He had told only

Birdy how he felt in his heart of hearts.

What made things worse was that Isla went into high-gear tourist season right around the same time. Tourist season and birthday got mixed up together in Pablo's mind, and it felt as if his entire town was celebrating something he didn't want to be reminded of.

But Emmanuel always said, "If you live in a place like Isla, you play to the crowd."

Right outside Pablo and Emmanuel's apartment windows, in fact, was a constant reminder of playing to the crowd. A slender steel cable stretched from an enormous hook just below their apartment all the way across the street, and on the cable hung a Seafarer painting silk-screened onto a huge banner. The painting, which was what Lula would call an "artist's rendering" of the mythical bird, rippled and flapped in the breeze. Sometimes Pablo and Birdy would stand at their bedroom window, looking out. On cloudless nights the giant painted parrot shone in the moonlight, its huge staring eyes visible to the boy and the bird in the window. It was a little creepy.

The cable ended across the street, just below a stone ledge on which perched a grotesque, a carved creature supposedly set there for protection. It was made of stone, a magnificent being unlike any animal or bird that Pablo had ever seen. Its enormous birdlike talons gripped the side of the brick building. It had a hunched, scaly back, large wings folded against its sides, hooded eyes that seemed to see in all directions at once, and a mouth that was half-open, revealing even stone teeth. Despite the fact that the grotesque never moved—it was made of stone, after all—it seemed almost alive to Pablo. Emmanuel agreed.

"The grotesque is another mythical beast," he said. "Some say that grotesques were once alive. That they lived here hundreds of years ago, thousands maybe, and that they're suspended now, neither fully alive nor fully dead."

"Why are they suspended?"

"To watch over the animals and birds of Isla.

To make sure that none of them end up like the grotesque, trapped, neither here nor there."

Pablo wasn't sure how he felt about the grotesque. On nights when they stood at the window, Birdy would press her head against the screen and look straight across at it. The grotesque seemed to be looking back at her, too. Its talons gripped the ledge and its body hunched over as if it had been caught and trapped just when it was about to fly. Birdy would shift from foot to foot, which was her sign of unease, when she looked at it.

"Maybe she thinks the grotesque is a bird too," Emmanuel said. "Another bird that can't fly, like her."

This didn't make sense to Pablo. The grotesque looked nothing like Birdy. But Birdy did seem fascinated by it. Sometimes, even on still nights, Pablo woke up to see her silhouetted against the window screen, staring out. When he called to her, she would flutter back to the suitcase. On those nights, Pablo would make himself stay awake until she drew one foot up and settled into sleep. Then he himself could finally close his eyes.

Pablo rocked himself to sleep every night. Emmanuel had figured out early on that his baby boy needed motion.

"My theory is that it's because you floated in on the waves," he said. "The ocean rocked you to sleep, and however long you were out there, you must have gotten used to it."

That was why there was no bed in Pablo's room. Instead Emmanuel had drilled two hooks into adjacent walls and strung a hammock woven from slender lengths of colorful rope from hook to hook. At night, Pablo stretched the hammock out and tipped himself and his blankets and his pillow into it. He pushed off with one hand and set it gently rocking. After a while, the motion of the swinging hammock felt like the rocking of a boat on the waves, and that was how he drifted off to sleep every night.

Birdy needed motion too. Even if she couldn't

fly, she loved it when Pablo almost-flew her down the beach on his shoulder or sailed her from room to room on his arm. She would lean forward a little, her talons digging in, and she never wanted him to stop.

The grotesque's building across the street was also home to a certain kind of swallow, who built nests under the overhang. To the right and left, below the grotesque's stone ledge, their intricate mud nests could be seen. Every year, Pablo and Birdy watched the baby swallows learn to fly. They were so tiny it was almost impossible to see them, black specks tumbling around in the air, their parents hovering nervously. The babies who survived flew farther and faster every day. Eventually they got to the point where they swooped around the grotesque, sometimes landing on its back, where they perched and rested.

Maria had consoled Pablo when he was younger and upset about the babies who didn't make it.

"It's part of the cycle of life," she told him.

"And it's hard to witness, like many things in nature. But there's a reason for all natural phenomena, whether we understand it or not."

Reason or not, it was hard to watch and harder to understand. Some things in life were like that. Like the idea of a baby launched alone into the ocean, with only a bird to keep him company.

TEN

PABLO WONDERED SOMETIMES about the huge storm that had swept through Isla just before he arrived. Was the storm the reason he'd been separated from whoever was with him? His hand came up and covered the necklace hidden beneath his T-shirt. For *someone* had to have been with him. Someone who had knotted the *Dios me bendiga* necklace around his neck, who had wrapped him in the green blanket and tied him so carefully into the little swimming pool.

"A few days before you arrived, during the

winds of change, there was that giant storm," Emmanuel had said. "And then came you. And look at you—Birdy, too—afraid of storms to this day."

Pablo *was* afraid of storms. A sky thick with darkening clouds, strong winds, rain that hammered down on the ceiling and woke him up at night: all these things filled him with fear. He would pull his knees to his chest in his hammock and wrap the blankets tight and try to make himself as small and invisible as possible, so the wind and the rain wouldn't find him. Even if animals had been allowed onboard the marine expedition, he wouldn't have wanted to go. What if a storm came up?

Birdy's fear was different. Her fear had to do with Pablo. When storms rolled in, when there was a threat of a hurricane, when the sky turned dark and ominous, Birdy would not leave Pablo's side even for a moment. She clung to his shoulder, his arm, the top of his head. She was ready with a swat if anyone else, even Emmanuel, came too close. She never slept at those times. For hours on end, an entire night, days even, she stayed awake and watchful, her eyes on Pablo.

The tourists were about to show up, and Pablo and Birdy were still on the bench outside Pierre's, late to help Emmanuel open up the store. Emmanuel counted on them in high season.

"Yikes, Birdy," Pablo said now. "We better get going."

Seafaring Souvenirs, like all the other shops except for Pierre's Goodies, opened promptly at ten a.m., just in time for the tourists to start arriving. Lula was chalking in her Tattoo of the Day special on the signboard outside Lula Tattoo.

Pablo was in a rush. But he stopped short when he saw the Tattoo of the Day, which looked to be a parrot soaring through the sky with wings spread wide, talons gripped around a baby in an inflatable swimming pool.

"What do you think, Pablo?" Lula said, standing back to admire her work.

What did Pablo think? He thought it was terrible, that's what he thought. Not because it was badly drawn—Lula was good at her renderings—but because, because . . .

"Lula, is that supposed to be *me*?"

"Yes! You and Birdy. It's an artist's rendering. Which means that—"

"I know what it means."

"Do you like it? I got the idea from—"

"I know where you got the idea from, Lula."

And he did. Every year it was Emmanuel's tradition to make up a new story to explain how Pablo had ended up in Isla. Last year, on Pablo's ninth non-birthday, he had come up with the Pablo-as-pirate-baby theory.

"Here's what I think," he had said. "You and Birdy were captives on a pirate ship that foundered on the rocks in a gigantic storm. The pirates forgot all about you because they were too busy running around on deck trying to save their treasure, and Birdy saw her chance."

Emmanuel pantomimed unspooling a coil of

rope, and then he made a series of invisible knots with quick arm movements.

"She lifted you up and put you into the little pool, then knotted you in tight with the twine."

"What would pirates be doing with a blow-up baby pool?" Pierre had asked.

"Pierre! Don't mess up a good story," Lula said.

"It's a reasonable question," Pierre said.

"They used it as a . . . a footbath," Emmanuel said. He was a fast thinker. "Pirates are known to enjoy a warm footbath at the end of a long day of plundering."

He had wiggled his toes, as if he himself were enjoying a warm footbath.

"Then, once the baby—that would be you, Pablo—was safely knotted into the pool, Birdy hauled you and the pool into the sky. And she started to fly."

A baby in a pool in the sky? That would be a heavy burden even for a bird of prey, which Birdy wasn't.

"I'm not sure that would be possible," Pablo said.

"And you would be correct," Emmanuel said. "Which is how Birdy, you, and the pool all came to rest upon the surface of the waves, where Birdy kept guard over you until you came floating in to shore, where a man—that would be me—found you and brought you home."

It was a good story, like most of Emmanuel's stories. Lula especially loved the pirate baby story, which explained why she was now re-creating part of it in her Tattoo of the Day.

"So what do you think?" she asked again.

I hate it, he thought. But he kept that thought, like the others, inside. His fingers reached up and closed over his necklace again. The pendant was solid and warm underneath his T-shirt.

"I'm giving it a test run," Lula said. "It's a possibility for your birthday tattoo."

Birdy jumped over to the chalkboard and gave the artist's rendering a swat.

"Birdy!" Lula said. "You don't like it?" She

looked from Birdy to Pablo in confusion, the chalk still in her hand. "Is something wrong, Pablo? You've been acting kind of weird lately."

But he just shook his head. Nothing was wrong. Except that something was, and he didn't know how to talk about it.

"It's not an ink tattoo," Lula said, still puzzled. "Just henna, gone in a week or so. Not something you'd be stuck with forever."

"I can think of a tattoo I'd want to be stuck with forever," Pablo said.

"Such as?"

"A Birdy tattoo."

"Oh, well. That's a different matter. Birdy's your best friend."

Birdy was more than a best friend. Much more. Pablo opened his mouth to say something, but a tourist—you could tell by the fact that he was wearing a Seafaring Parrot sun hat—holding a bakery bag wanted Lula's attention.

"Excuse me, miss?" the man said, gesturing with his free hand toward the Tattoo of the Day.

"Is that a Seafaring Parrot, by chance?"

"It's an artist's rendering of what a Seafarer might look like," Lula said, "since no one really knows what a—" but then there was a commotion and she didn't finish her sentence.

ELEVEN

THE LITTLE DOG snuck down the alley to where it opened onto the bright sidewalk. The noise of the street beyond, which had been muffled by the narrowness of the alley and the buildings that rose on either side, was much louder here. Cars puttered by in the wake of a double-decker bus. Passersby meandered along, their chatter indistinct.

Now he was at the very end of the alleyway.

He hunched against the taller brick building and nosed his head out, the better to see. He slanted his eyes to the right. A woman was standing in front of a board of some kind with a piece of chalk in her hand. She was drawing a picture of a strange bird carrying a strange something through the air.

The dog slanted his eyes to the left. There was the sound of a door opening and closing, and—

—ohhhhh—

—the most delicious smell he had ever smelled came wafting into his poking-out nose. Butter and cinnamon and sugar and everything that was good in the world. He closed his eyes, the better to smell the heavenly smell. Closer and closer and closer it came, until he opened his eyes and saw a hand holding a white waxed paper bag. The hand and the bag were only a few feet away from the dog's nose. The heavenly smell was coming from the bag. The person holding the bag had stopped to talk with the woman holding the chalk.

Look at the heavenly bag, just dangling there,

right there in front of him. Right at the level of his jaws.

The dog slunk forward just an inch. Then just another inch.

Could he?

Should he?

Would he?

TWELVE

“GOOD HEAVENS!” SHOUTED the tattoo-inquiring tourist in the Seafaring Parrot sun hat. “I've been robbed of my elephant ears!”

“Robbed?” said Lula.

“Elephant ears?” said Pablo.

“Didn't you see? Just now! A thief just snatched my bakery bag!”

“Thief?” said Lula and Pablo together.

The robbery had happened so fast that none of them, not even the tourist, was exactly sure what had just taken place.

"One minute I was standing here talking to you, holding my bag of elephant ears," the tourist said, "and the next thing I knew, the bag had been ripped from my hand."

He turned in a circle, peering up and down the street. "It just disappeared," he said. "Right out of my hand."

He looked sadly at Pablo and Lula and Pierre, who had come out of the bakery at the sound of the commotion.

"I've been hearing about Pierre's famous elephant ears for years," he said.

"They *are* famous," agreed Pierre. "Justly so, I might add. I trained in Paris, you know."

"Pierre," said Lula, with a significant look, nodding toward the bakery. "Do you have any elephant ears left?"

"Mais oui!" said Pierre. "Allow me to supply you, sir, with another bag of elephant ears. On the house," he added, after another look from Lula. "We do not tolerate thievery in our town."

When the tourist had been resupplied with

elephant ears and sent on his way, Lula and Pablo and Pierre looked at one another. A thief? In Isla? It was practically unheard of.

"Well, let's hope that's the end of that," said Lula.

"Indeed," said Pierre. "A rash of unsolved crimes would not be good publicity for Isla."

Pablo didn't know what to think. It had all happened in an instant: Lula talking about the tattoo with the man in the sun hat, the white bag dangling from his hand, everything ordinary and unremarkable, and then *WHOOSH*, there had been a blur and a yell and *WHOOSH*, the bag was gone and no one knew where it went. Very strange.

Pablo and Birdy hurried to the store. Emmanuel had already opened up for the day, just in time for the first wave of double-decker bus passengers. Pablo took up his station at the cash register and began ringing up the T-shirts, the souvenir mugs and maps and pens and hats and Pablo's Painted Parrots. Over the years,

Emmanuel too had suggested that Pablo might want to expand his repertoire of Pablo's Painted Parrots.

"Tourists love the Seafarer," he said. "You might—"

"No," said Pablo.

"But a man's got to make a living, right?"

"No."

The tourists would have to make do with Pablo's renderings of Sugar Baby, Peaches, and Mr. Chuckles. And Rhody the rooster, of course. Sometimes, if there weren't too many customers, Pablo set up his painting table and sunshade on the sidewalk and went to work. The repetitive strokes of the tiny brush on the shells were soothing. Tourists occasionally stopped to watch him, but he didn't mind because they kept their distance. What he did mind was when the Committee stopped by and took turns fluttering up to the level of the table, as if to critique his work.

"Hmm." That was Mr. Chuckles's usual comment, even though Pablo privately thought that his paintings of Mr. Chuckles were extremely flattering. He made Mr. Chuckles look quite noble, in fact. Certainly better than the bird on the Seafaring Parrot banner.

WELCOME TO ISLA, HOME OF THE LEGENDARY SEAFARING PARROT! read the caption. The strange-looking parrot-ish bird on the banner was really starting to bother Pablo. He wasn't alone.

"What *is* that thing?" Lula had said when the banner was first hung up.

"I believe it's what you would call an artist's rendering," said Pierre. "The free market at work."

"It's called capitalism," said Emmanuel.

"It's called ugly," said Pablo.

And it was. They all agreed. There was something about the eyes on the banner bird. They were too burning. And one wing was raised in a military sort of salute. But the tourists didn't mind. They were eager for any scrap of information about the mythical bird, which led to lots of questions, none of which could really be answered, because no one had ever seen an actual Seafarer in real life. Question after question, not all of which were about birds.

"Little boy, can you tell me where the famous elephant-ear bakery is?"

"Little boy, can you tell me where's the nearest restroom?"

"Little boy, is there some place around here that sells"—Band-Aids, soda, parrot T-shirts, coconut candy, sun hats, beach umbrellas—you name it, the tourists wanted it. They tumbled off the double-decker bus and they tumbled in and out of shops and they took up the whole sidewalk.

Some of the tourists wanted to take photos of Birdy perched on Pablo's shoulder.

"I'm sorry, no photos allowed."

"But why not?"

Because Birdy is not a tourist act, Pablo would think, but he never said anything. He just shook his head politely and went back to his work. Some of them even tried to pet Birdy. *Pet* her! As if she were a dog or a kitten instead of a bird. Birds weren't made to be petted, at least by strangers, but the tourists didn't seem to know that.

"Oh, can I pet your bird?"

"I'm sorry, she doesn't like to be petted."

"What kind of bird is she?"

"She's a parrot."

"Is she a Seafaring Parrot?"

"Well, no one really knows what a Seafaring Parrot actually looks like."

Or if they even exist, Pablo would add, but only in his head. Everyone wanted to believe in the existence of the Seafaring Parrot.

Of all the people who wanted to believe in the Seafaring Parrot, the one who most wanted to believe was Elmira Toledo. She was a frequent presence on the tiny television that Pierre kept in the bakery next to his dough-mixing counter. He claimed that the television was there to keep track of the weather, but more than once Pablo had come upon Pierre watching cartoons, with the television turned low so that only he could hear it, while he mixed and kneaded dough.

Next morning Elmira was front and center on the screen.

"Today we bring you the first of an in-depth series," she began, looking into the camera over the tops of her purple glasses, "on a subject near and dear to many hearts. Namely, the Seafaring Parrot."

Reporters were not uncommon in town. They all hoped to get the scoop on any and all Seafaring Parrot news, but Elmira outshone the others. She had been sniffing out Seafaring Parrot stories ever since the winds of change last blew, at the time of Pablo's arrival. Out at sea, fishermen had reported a parrotlike bird riding the waves on a piece of debris.

Years ago, Elmira had set up something she called the Toledo Tip Line, on which anyone who thought they'd seen a Seafarer could leave a message. She personally followed up with each caller. Most she termed "attention seekers," whose descriptions of the bird so perfectly matched the encyclopedia speculation of what a Seafaring Parrot looked like that they were immediately discredited.

Once in a while, though, there was a report that made her pause, narrow her eyes, and take a second or third look.

There had been several such reports the day before Pablo's arrival, sightings that were, in the words of Elmira, "more credible than most." She summarized the sightings every year, and this year was no exception.

"Oh, here we go again," said Lula, who harbored an intense dislike of Elmira.

"It's that time of year," said Pierre. "The return of the Toledo."

"Summary my foot," Lula muttered. "That's just a fancy way of saying 'I don't have anything new to report, so I'm just going to roll out the same old thing again.'"

On the television, Elmira, her trademark trench coat blowing in the breeze, was standing on the shore of a beach. It wasn't their beach, but she didn't bother to mention that.

"Nearly ten years ago there were several reports, by fishermen, of a Seafaring Parrot just off the beach of Isla," she said, gesturing with her non-microphone arm, "reports that were, in my opinion, credible enough to warrant yearly follow-up."

The camera panned upward for a panoramic shot of the blue sky, a few wispy clouds and seagulls in sight.

"Several calls to the Toledo Tip Line all reported the same thing," Elmira continued, "which was the strange sight of a lone Seafarer riding the waves on a piece of floating debris, which might have been a piece of driftwood, a raft, or, in the words of the last caller, 'some kind of boogie board.'"

Photos scrolled by on the screen: shots of a piece of driftwood, a whitewater raft complete with paddles, and a beach supplies store with boogie boards in the front window.

"She's tenacious," said Pierre. "I'll give her that."

"She's a pit bull," said Lula.

The yearly summary was tiresome enough, but what was more tiresome was Elmira herself, in the flesh, showing up with her camera crew year after year right around Pablo's non-birthday. That was a dreaded event.

"There were even rumors that an actual specimen might have landed on the shores of Isla," Elmira said. "But despite multiple credible sightings, the legend remains just that: a legend. Mystery wrapped in riddle, bound up in longing. And now, speaking of mystery, let me turn things over to our weatherman, Darren Mandible, who has exciting news."

Darren Mandible had strong feelings about the weather, especially when it came to southernmost regions like Isla. He was fixated on wind, especially the winds of change. If there was a remote possibility that the winds of Isla would shift to straight onshore or offshore, Darren Mandible went into high gear. He usually wore a white suit and kept his gray hair in a long, skinny ponytail, and when things got exciting, he had a habit of dipping and bending and spinning around his television weather map. Pablo was pretty sure that it wasn't the weather Pierre liked to keep track of so much as Darren Mandible and his dramatic delivery.

"This is Darren Mandible with a *special* weather report for our *southernmost* region. Oh my, viewers, what do we have here now?" Darren dipped onto one knee to point at Isla on the map. "A tropical storm coalescing within striking range of our favorite parrot town?" Here he swooped up, his long ponytail flapping. "Could this possibly be a harbinger of the winds . . . of . . . *change*?"

Lula and Pierre and Pablo and Emmanuel were all silent. The winds of change hadn't been seen in Isla for nearly ten years.

"Isla residents, keep your eyes peeled," Darren ended. "Because we all know what the winds of change portend, do we not?"

They did. Pierre clicked the television off.

No one said anything for a minute. The winds of change portended only two things. One was the possibility of a Seafaring Parrot landing in their town. The other was the possibility of a Seafaring Parrot leaving their town. Both possibilities filled Pablo with wonder, along with relief that Birdy wasn't a Seafarer. But the old fisherman's saying ran through Pablo's mind, and he was pretty sure it was running through everyone else's mind too. *The winds of change mean fortune lost or fortune gained.*

THIRTEEN

"HAS THE PASTRY thief been found?" said Emmanuel.

Pablo shook his head. It had been two days, but the robbery of the elephant ears remained an unsolved case. The bike cops had ridden up and down all the neighboring streets, asking questions and searching for an abandoned bakery bag. But no one had seen anything, and there were so many bakery bags crumpled up in the trash cans that the bike cops gave up trying to find evidence. There hadn't been a recurrence of the crime, though, so maybe the thief was long gone.

Pablo could hear the first of the buses grumbling its way toward their block. He bent over the display of Pablo's Painted Parrots, rearranging them. Yesterday someone had bought a Rhody shell and asked what the special characteristics of a Chicken Parrot were, and whether the Chicken Parrot bore any resemblance to a Seafaring Parrot. Pablo didn't feel like going through that again, so he was putting all the Rhody shells in the back, where they would be less visible.

Emmanuel sorted through the ones and fives and tens and twenties in the cash drawer. He printed WE NEED ONES! THANKS! on a piece of scrap paper and taped it to the register. Then he put both hands on the counter and studied them, as if there were something on his mind, and looked up at Pablo.

"Listen, Pablo. I've been thinking about something."

Oh no, thought Pablo. *Here it comes.* What did

he want to do for his birthday? Double digits. Et cetera.

"You're coming up on double digits now," said Emmanuel, and Pablo braced himself. "And there's something I want to talk to you about"—but then there was a disturbance in the ranks of the Committee. Mr. Chuckles was trying to horn in on a piece of coconut given to Peaches by a tourist. This wasn't going over well with Peaches.

"Hey! Watch what you're saying!"

"HAHAHAHAHA!"

"Shoo," said Emmanuel. "All of you. Go look for trouble somewhere else." They reluctantly groused their way out the door, and off down the sidewalk they went. Emmanuel took a breath and looked down at his hands again, but Pablo dreaded a birthday question, so he interrupted with the first thing that came into his head.

"What do you think of Lula's chalkboard?"

Lula had come up with a whole new idea that she referred to as a public art project. This consisted of an enormous chalkboard set up outside

Lula Tattoo, empty but for one large chalked question—

> If you could bring back
> any voice in the world,
> which one would YOU bring back?

—along with an assortment of colored chalk, so passersby could write in their answers. The tourists had taken to the public art project right away. From Pablo's spot at the cash register, or outside at his painting table by the T-shirt racks, he could watch as they stopped at the big chalkboard, picked up a piece of chalk, and thought for a minute before writing down a name. Most of them were alike.

> Mahatma Gandhi
> Harriet Tubman
> Jesus Christ
> Amelia Earhart
> Abraham Lincoln

Martin Luther King Jr.

The Prophet Muhammad

Susan B. Anthony

Sacagawea

All these were famous people, important people. Pablo supposed that it would be interesting to hear their voices, what they had sounded like, what they had to say. Maybe listen to some of the famous speeches or quotes.

"The one-question chalkboard?" Emmanuel said. "It's popular. I'll give it that."

He looked at Pablo and cleared his throat, as if he had something important to say. But Pablo kept his eyes on the painted shells and his hands busy organizing them.

"But what about you, Emmanuel? If you could bring back any voice, which one would you bring back?"

"Well. That would take some thought, I guess. There's a lot to choose from."

A wave of tourists came flooding into the store

just then—the double-decker bus's first load of the day—and Emmanuel turned to greet them. Phew. Pablo had managed to avert another birthday question, at least for a while. But Lula's chalkboard had made him think. If he, Pablo, could pick just one person's voice to bring back, he wouldn't choose anyone famous. He wouldn't choose anyone from the depths of history. He wouldn't even choose anyone whose name he knew.

"You know who I would write down on that board?" Pablo whispered into Birdy's ear while Emmanuel was busy greeting the customers.

She pushed her beak into his neck, which meant *Tell me.*

"It's a secret. You can't tell anyone."

Which was a crazy thing to say to a bird who had never told anyone anything, but it was part of his routine. She pushed harder. *Tell me.*

"My mother," he whispered. "Even though I don't know my mother's name. Even though I don't know if I even had a mother."

This time she pushed so hard that it almost

hurt. As if she was trying to tell him that everyone had a mother. Everyone. Even babies who floated in all by themselves on the tide, with only a bird to watch over them.

FOURTEEN

THE DOG EDGED along the backs of the buildings until he was again close to the end of the alley. The light grew steadily brighter as he approached the sidewalk and the street beyond. The shadows of humans preceded the humans themselves, and so did the sound of their voices.

"Can we get some ice cream?"

"Can I have a T-shirt?"

"I need to go pee!"

"Wait wait, I left my camera back at the restaurant!"

"Did you see that bird? Is that a parrot?"

"Mom! Dad! Is that a *Seafaring Parrot*?"

On and on they went, the voices, the shadows, the people themselves. They all walked right past the narrow opening to the alley, as if they didn't see it. The dog huddled as close as possible to the last building. It was made of brick and it felt cool against his matted fur. Another shadow was coming, a strange-looking one. The little dog hadn't seen one quite like it before. It looked to be a human shadow, maybe a child because it was short, but there was something unusual about one of the shadow's arms—it stuck up and out in a weird way. Kind of like his own once-broken tail.

Curious, the dog sidled forward, forward, forward—

—Oh! He backed up just in time, because the curious shadow turned out to be a bird and a boy. The bird was perched on the boy's arm, and they walked right past the opening to the alley. The boy didn't see the dog, huddled and small against the cool brick.

But the bird was another matter entirely. She turned, and her eyes found the young dog's eyes. He pressed himself as skinny as he could against the brick, but there was no hiding from that bird.

She looked right at him and his head filled up with noise.

Staticky noise: voices, laughter, shrieks.

Wind and rain and groans of something not human, something that sounded like wood being torn apart.

All this the young dog heard in the span of a few seconds, as the bird on the boy's arm passed him by. He had never experienced anything like it. All that noise, unfamiliar and unsettling.

The growling in his stomach, though, that was familiar. A moment later the dog slunk forward until he was just inches from the bright light of the sidewalk and the street beyond. So many, many food smells. And among them the same smell from the other day, of butter and sugar and cinnamon. Oh, that smell. The strange bird was forgotten in an instant in favor of food. Food. *Food.* The little dog drooled long ropes of saliva. His stomach rumbled and moaned.

Should he?

Could he?

Would he?

FIFTEEN

NEXT DAY WAS SUNDAY, and the Committee lagged behind Mr. Chuckles, who was in top form, with all the churchgoers to critique. He even attempted to pass judgment on Pablo and Birdy, who were on their way back from the beach with a basketful of new shells for Pablo to paint. Mr. Chuckles leaned out of the box elder tree by the church, looked them up and down, and opened his beak in a HAHAHAHAHA-like manner. But Birdy raised her wing in warning, and Mr. Chuckles must have thought better of whatever he was about to say, because he turned back to the churchgoers.

"Hmm."

"Nice threads!"

"Hmm."

"Hmm."

It was a morning heavy on *hmms*. No one had gotten a Mr. Chuckles *HAHAHAHAHA*, at least not yet anyway, but Pablo had the distinct feeling that the judge needed to be stopped before things got out of hand.

"Come on, Mr. Chuckles," he said. "Come on, Committee. The Sunday show is over. Back to work now."

"Simmer down, simmer down," squawked Peaches, as if she were agreeing. Or maybe disagreeing. It wasn't always easy to tell.

Back to work they went, Birdy clinging to Pablo's arm, swaying back and forth as they walked. Rhody was distracted by an ear of corn by a garbage can. He would peck at it, look up to see the Committee far ahead, hurry to catch up with them, then remember the ear of corn and head back to it. It was slow going.

They were nearly at Pierre's, all of them, when Mr. Chuckles stopped at the entrance to the alley halfway down the block. He stood there as if he were looking for something.

"Come on, Mr. Chuckles," said Pablo, "don't stop now. We've come so far."

But Mr. Chuckles was fixated on whatever was in the alleyway. He extended his head and took a cautious hop forward, and then—

—a wild-eyed dog darted out of the alleyway, leaped right over Mr. Chuckles, and headed straight toward the rest of them. He increased his speed as he got closer, a lopsided brush of a tail pluming out behind him, and then skidded to a halt in front of Pierre's Goodies before charging straight on in, straight behind the counter, and then—before Pierre could even get to his feet—straight out again he came, his mouth full of elephant ears. Pablo managed to count two, no, three, no, four, wait, FIVE, elephant ears in the dog's jaws before he veered right, hurdled over Peaches, who was too shocked to squawk, and then zoomed away down the sidewalk.

Pierre was outside now.

"Halt, thief!" he yelled. "Bring back those pastries! GET THAT DOG!"

The dog was almost at the end of the block now, bits of elephant ear flying behind him, and Pierre took off after him.

"I never saw that man run so fast," said Lula, who had come sprinting out of her store mid-tattoo, cone of henna clutched in her hand, a half-tattooed tourist trailing behind her.

Pablo didn't think he'd ever seen Pierre run at all. Birdy leaped to Pablo's shoulder and dug her talons in deep. All four of them stared as Pierre rounded the corner at the end of the block, still shouting after the dog, with Peaches joining in.

"Halt, thief! Halt, I say!"

"Simmer down now! Simmer down!"

The ruckus attracted a small crowd, including the double-decker bus, which ground to a halt next to the bakery. Tourists in sun hats peered from the open windows. Birdy, Pablo, Lula, and the Committee watched as Pierre came trudging back around the corner, his chef hat in his hand. No dog in sight.

"Well," said Lula, "at least we know who the pastry thief is."

"Who," said Pierre, panting with exertion. "We know who, but not where. The thief has disappeared."

He plopped his chef hat onto his head.

"Pierre will find that thief," he said. "And Pierre will make him pay!"

"Where in the world did that dog come from?" said Lula.

"Out of there, I think," said Pablo, and he pointed to the alleyway. "He jumped right over Mr. Chuckles and Peaches."

Mr. Chuckles appeared stunned by what had happened, but not for long. He gathered his wits about him and opened his beak.

"HAHAHAHAHA! NICE THREADS! HMM!

HAHAHAHAHA! NICE THREADS! HMM! HAHAHAHAHA! HMM! HMM! HMM!"

There was a manic gleam in his eye, as if all the words he knew were jumbling up in his head after the fright. It took a head butt from Peaches to make him stop. They were all a little stunned at the speed of the robbery. Dogs were common in Isla, but they were usually well-fed, well-loved lazy dogs on leashes. This was a stealth dog. A dog that looked as if it were starving. A dog that was no doubt somewhere nearby right now, even if none of them knew where, wolfing down Pierre's elephant ears. *Poor little guy,* thought Pablo.

"Maybe he belongs to one of the tourists," said Lula.

"Maybe he got lost off a fishing boat," said the flower lady.

"Maybe he escaped from prison," said Pierre. "That would explain a few things."

SIXTEEN

THE DOG GALLOPED along so fast, down the sidewalk and around the block, that he almost missed the alley entrance. At the last minute he caught sight of its dark opening and flung himself into it. Halfway down the alley, just outside the back door to the Parrot Café, he slowed and then stopped. His sides were heaving and he still had a mouthful of half-chewed elephant ear. He swallowed it down, licked his chops, then bent and licked the top of his right paw, where some of the sugary crumbs were caught.

Now *that* was a meal.

His belly, for the first time in weeks, wasn't hurting from hunger. Oh, he was still hungry. Make no mistake about that. But the immediate ache, the pains of starvation that had stabbed through him the last few days, were at bay.

He could still see the surprise in the eyes of the first bird, the one he'd leaped over on his way out of the alley, and the shock in the eyes of the second bird, the one he'd leaped over on his way down the sidewalk.

There had been a chicken, too, somewhere in the mix. Chickens were tasty. He knew this from a chicken bone he had once found in an overturned garbage can. Not as tasty as elephant ears, but not bad. Not bad at all.

The strange bird had been there too, perched on the boy's arm, the bird who had looked straight at him when he was hiding in the alley. The bird whose outside was silent and whose inside was full of voices and shrieks and laughter and whispers and songs and screams.

The silent bird was so full of noise. So, much, noise.

The dog lay down in the dust and concrete, against the cool brick wall of the building that housed the café. He could smell the kitchen from here. Through the closed steel door, the smells of cooking came wafting. Oh, those glorious smells.

Tortilla soup.

Chicken mole.

Quesadillas.

Voices came faintly through the locked door too, voices of the chef and the sous-chef and the line cooks and the bussers and servers and dishwasher. Talking, laughing, teasing one another. The voices sounded as if they belonged to busy, happy people. People who liked one another. People who worked together, cooked together, ate together, belonged together. More smells now.

Flan.

Guacamole.

And more quesadillas, cheese quesadillas with

onion and cilantro and cheese, glorious cheese melting over the crisped edges of corn tortillas, glorious corn tortillas with *queso fresco* and *pico de gallo*. Oh, those cheese quesadillas.

The elephant ears were already a distant memory. How the dog wanted one of those quesadillas. Or two. Three, maybe. Possibly six or seven.

SEVENTEEN

IN THE EARLY mornings, as they sat in the bakery with their coffee and pastries, Emmanuel and Lula and Pierre had long argued over whose theories about Pablo and Birdy's arrival were more likely to be correct.

"Here's my theory," said Pierre, balancing an elephant ear on the tip of his index finger. It was the day after the robbery. "There is the map of the world, the one that we all know. Picture it in your minds." He sketched the outline of the continents in the air with his non-elephant-ear hand. "There is North America, South America. There is Europe—see, right here is France, *la belle France*—there is the African continent, there is the Asian continent. There is Australia, there is the South Pole, there is the North Pole, there are all the little islands in all the large seas. This is the map of the world as we know it."

He stood in front of them, the elephant ear tipping this way and that.

"But consider the following," Pierre went on. "What if the map of the world as we know it is missing a few countries?"

He gestured with his non-elephant-ear hand in the direction of the sea.

"Surely it is possible," he said. "How could one ever know all the countries there are in the world? The hugeness of the sea, the tininess of our eyes."

He turned back and looked at Pablo and Birdy, his gaze solemn. "Which brings me to my theory, which is that you came from a country not yet discovered by outsiders, whose people sent you and the bird as emissaries. Emissaries from the forgotten world."

So enthralled was Pierre with his story that he inadvertently clasped his hands together, sending the elephant ear flying to the floor.

"Mon dieu!" said Pierre.

He picked up the elephant ear, gave it a quick inspection, looked sadly at the spot on the floor where it had landed, and then took a bite.

"As I was saying," he said through the crumbs, "it is my firm belief that you are both emissaries from a world as yet unknown. Undiscovered. A world where miracles can still happen, as evidenced by the fact that you came floating up to our shore on that hallowed day."

Pierre's story was a good one. An undiscovered country, one unknown to the rest of the world? Maybe the inhabitants there lived in tree houses, or underground.

"Pierre's theory is a bit different from mine," said Lula. "I believe that our Pablo's appearance in Isla is the result of his precocity."

Pierre looked at her with narrowed eyes. Pablo suspected that he was trying to cover up the fact that he, like Pablo, didn't know what the word "precocity" meant.

"Consider the facts," she said, ticking them off on her fingers. "We have a baby. We have a bird. We have a small swimming pool meant for backyard use, certainly not on the open ocean."

Everyone nodded, including the sous-chef from the Parrot Café, who was hurrying by with his take-out coffee and not even part of the conversation. Even Peaches and Sugar Baby, who had hustled over to the scene of the elephant-ear mishap and were pecking at some crumbs, looked up and cocked their heads.

"Hmm," said Mr. Chuckles, but everyone ignored him.

"Now consider the following scenario," said Lula, holding up her hand for emphasis. "A party. Perhaps a *Feliz Navidad* party. Old people, young people, middle-aged people, dogs and cats, music, everyone milling about. Babies laughing. Or screaming."

She grimaced. Lula wasn't a fan of babies. The very idea of babies exhausted her. Some people were like that.

"And in the middle of the party, at the height of the merriment, just as the gifts were about to be distributed, one baby crawled away," said Lula. "One *precocious* baby."

Pierre frowned again, possibly because he, like Pablo, didn't know the meaning of "precocious" any more than he knew the meaning of "precocity."

"That one very special baby," continued Lula, "had other things in mind. What was a *Navidad* party to that baby? Nada. No, no, he had a master plan for the day. A master plan"—here she looked from one to another—"that involved a little swimming pool in the backyard of the home where the party was being held."

Everyone was nodding now, picturing the little swimming pool.

"The precocious baby looked around, saw that everyone else was focused on the festivities, and seized his chance. Out the back door he snuck, grabbed the swimming pool between his gums, and crawled his way straight to the beach, where he set sail. And the rest," Lula added, "is history."

Birdy was staring at Lula as if she had left out something essential. Which, of course, she had.

"What about the bird?" asked Pierre.

"The bird?" said Lula. "Oh yes, the bird. The bird, let's see, the bird . . . decided to come along for the ride."

She brushed her hands together in a *that's it* sort of way. Birdy raised her wing, but Pablo quickly scooped her up before she could give Lula a swat. Lula's story, even if she had nearly forgotten to include Birdy, was a good one too. The only problem was that no one knew if either story were true.

Lula turned to Emmanuel with an expectant look.

"Your turn," she said, and she settled back in her chair. Emmanuel's stories were usually the best, because they were the most far-fetched. Take the pirate baby story from last year, for example. The idea of a pirate baby crawling around on the deck of a pirate ship could even make Pablo smile. But Emmanuel just glanced at Pablo, a troubled look in his eyes, and shook his head.

"No story?" Pierre said, disappointed. "But yours are the best."

"Not today," said Emmanuel. "Not today."

EIGHTEEN

THAT NIGHT, PABLO had one of his ocean dreams. Ocean dreams came each year around his non-birthday. Each of them began with Pablo rocking on the waves, flat on his back, looking up at the sky above. Birdy's talons blocked his view, and he reached up to push them aside, but she wouldn't budge. Baby Pablo, unbudging Birdy. Ocean waves gentle below them both, rocking them like a giant watery rocking chair.

They didn't end that way, though.

In one dream, the waves grew bigger and

bigger and bigger, until finally they splashed over the edge of the swimming pool and it began to sink. Pablo always woke up just as he was going under.

That was a terrible dream.

In another, the sky turned darker and darker and darker. Pablo could see nothing, nothing at all—not even Birdy—until the moon rose high enough to shine soft light down on them both. In this dream, he and Birdy rocked their way through the night.

That was a good dream.

In another one, the waves were big and swift underneath the tiny swimming pool. Too big, too swift. Baby Pablo rose and fell, rose and fell, and Birdy's talons shifted. It was hard for her to hold on. There were voices in the background, shouting and panicked. Then they faded.

Another bad dream. This one went on and on, one of those strange dreams that Pablo, even though he was asleep, knew he was having. That happened sometimes, with his ocean dreams, and he had never been able to wake himself up from them. Tonight was different, though. Tonight, a voice woke him up.

"Pablo. Pobrecito Pablo."

It was the same voice! The woman's voice that he had heard before. Pablo sat up in his hammock.

"Birdy? Did you hear that?"

But again, she was sound asleep, her head tucked into her feathers. Had the voice just been part of the ocean dream? Pablo lay awake, wondering and listening, for a long time. When the sky began to grow light, he pedaled down to the shore with Birdy in the basket. It was early enough that no one would be around to talk to him or possibly ask about his birthday. The members of the Committee were still roosting. There hadn't even been a single crow from Rhody. Maybe, in his ongoing attempt to turn himself into a parrot, he was forcing himself not to crow.

"Here's the thing, Birdy," Pablo said when they reached the beach. "I don't want to hear any more made-up stories about you and me and how we got here."

Birdy fluttered down from Pablo's arm and stood on the sand at his feet, lifting her wings so the breeze could ruffle her feathers. A piece of driftwood tumbled about in the lapping waves, and she cocked her head as if it were a fish that needed to be watched.

"Remember when Maria asked me if I had plans for my birthday and I told her I was going to do something brave? I don't know why I said that."

He thought about the little dog. Even if he was a pastry thief, the little dog was a brave pastry thief. Look at the way he had practically flown over Mr. Chuckles and Peaches in his desperate attempt to make off with the elephant ears.

"I mean, what could *I* do that's brave?" Pablo said.

He felt for his necklace and closed his fingers around it. Birdy was listening, as always.

"Every one of their stories makes me sound

brave. Pirate baby, precocious baby, messenger from another world. But none of those stories are true."

Pablo himself had a few theories about how he ended up on the ocean.

Theory #1. Maybe his original parents, whoever they had been, had taken him to the beach and put him in the little swimming pool to keep him safe. Sort of like a little playpen. But then they had fallen asleep, in the hot sun, and no one had noticed when the tide came up and carried the baby in the tiny swimming pool out to sea.

Theory #2. Maybe, when his parents had fallen asleep one day, he had woken up from his nap and crawled right out of the house and down to the ocean, where he had found an abandoned tiny swimming pool, gotten into it, and paddled out to sea.

Theory #3. Maybe Pablo had been a difficult baby, one of those babies who screamed all the time and never stopped, their red faces always squinched up and bellowing. The kind of baby that drove Lula insane. There were lots of babies like that. Pablo had seen them in the store, squalling in their strollers, their parents exhausted and at their wits' end. Maybe he had been one of those babies. Maybe his parents just hadn't been able to take it anymore, so they had pushed him out to sea in a tiny swimming pool and waved good-bye.

Pablo didn't like this theory. Or any of them, really. But sometimes he couldn't help wondering where he had come from and how he'd gotten here, at this time of year especially, when the ocean dreams descended. Or when he woke up in the middle of the night and everything was quiet and still except for Birdy, dreaming in her sleep, perched there on the old Cuba suitcase and sighing. Was there another theory, one he hadn't figured out yet?

"Come on, Birdy-bird," he said. "Let's go see Maria."

Maria was a scientist. She believed in facts. And she knew how to keep a confidence. The clinic wasn't officially open yet, but when Maria saw who it was, she unlocked the door and let them into the empty waiting room. This was her open door policy, which applied only to Pablo and Birdy. He got right to the point.

"Maria, is it really true that sound doesn't ever disappear? Every sound ever made is still out there?"

"Not really. Sounds last longer than we can hear them, but even loud sounds eventually disappear."

"And human ears can only hear sounds when they happen?"

"Unless you count hearing them in your head, in memory," Maria said. "Which I don't. Human memory does not represent scientific proof, and my nature is that of a scientist."

"Well, is there any way to sharpen our ears?" said Pablo. "So that we *could* hear sounds from the past?"

"Not that I know of. Why?"

"Well," he began, "I've heard this voice. Twice

now. In the middle of the night. But I can't figure out if I'm hearing it for real or if it's just a dream."

"What does the voice say?"

"My name. Pablo. Actually, *pobrecito Pablo*."

Maria looked at him thoughtfully. She reached out and brushed his hair out of his eyes, the way that Emmanuel did. The gesture loosened Pablo's tongue.

"I don't want any more fake stories," he said. He was on the verge of tears, which embarrassed him, but he kept going. "I want my real story, the whole story. I only know the part that begins here, when we came floating in on the waves."

"I don't blame you. I would wonder too, if I were you."

"Everyone makes those stories up," said Pablo. "They act as though the truth doesn't matter."

"It does matter, though," said Maria. "You were a someone before you were set upon the waves. You were a someone, and . . ."

"And what?"

"And someone was watching over you. Someone wanted you to live."

Pablo thought about that. It must be true. Someone had tried to keep him safe. But in some ways, knowing that fact made not knowing his whole story that much worse.

"Maria? Do you ever wish you had the ears of a Seafaring Parrot?"

"No," she said immediately. "Never. I think it would be a very hard life. Some stories are hard to hear, Pablo. And knowing every one of them would be a hard burden to bear."

"It's better to hear them anyway," Pablo argued.

"Maybe." Maria regarded him with her kind and thoughtful eyes. "And maybe not."

NINETEEN

PABLO WOKE UP that night, restless. It was windy, and the Seafaring Parrot banner was flapping. He got out of his hammock and pressed his face against the window screen and watched it curling and uncurling. Like waves on the beach. It was unsettling to wake up and see the giant parrot hanging there in midair. He wished its eyes weren't quite so bright and burning. Couldn't the painter have made it a little less creepy-looking, especially when no one knew what the bird looked like, or if it was even real?

Here was what *was* real:

Pablo's *Dios me bendiga* necklace, which he had never taken off.

Birdy, who had never left his side.

The tiny swimming pool, deflated and stored on the shelf in his closet.

The green blanket, washed and folded and kept next to the pool.

Those things were absolutely, verifiably real. Everything else that surrounded his arrival in Isla—Lula's precocious-baby theory, Pierre's emissary-from-a-forgotten-world theory, Emmanuel's pirate-baby theory, the day that they had arbitrarily picked for his birthday—all that was made up out of thin air.

But in a way, thin air was real, wasn't it? The baby birds across the street tumbled out of their nests into it, and they spread their wings and it held them up. The lucky ones, that is. Birds knew that the air was real, and they trusted it enough to fling themselves onto it and spread their wings.

Something could be invisible and still exist.

Even Maria, with her scientific nature, couldn't argue with that.

Birdy was sleeping on the old suitcase, her head tucked under her feathers and one foot drawn up. Across the street, the grotesque's eyes were dark caves against his stone body. The steel cable shone in the moonlight. The painted parrot's eyes glowed up at Pablo.

"I'm sick of artists' renderings," whispered Pablo. "They're all fakes."

He raised the screen an inch at a time so as not to wake Birdy. When it was high enough, he stuck his head out and looked down, down, down at the street below. It was empty this late at night. All the stores were closed and locked, all the lights turned off. Even the Parrot Café, which was always the last place to close, was shuttered and dark.

Sugar Baby and Rhody and Mr. Chuckles and Peaches were asleep in their roosts and nests. The pigeons and doves and random chickens and wild parrots who fluttered about busily during the day were all silent too. There was nothing moving on the entire street. Even the baby birds were asleep in the mud nests that clung to the underside of the grotesque's stone ledge across the street.

Pablo was sure that he was the only living being awake in the entire town of Isla, and he—

Wait, what was that?

Something was moving down below.

A shape, almost indistinguishable in the shadows, was making its way along the sidewalk. Whatever it was—too big to be a mouse or a cat or even a sleepless chicken—it was trying to stay inconspicuous, huddled up against the sides of the buildings. Slipping along without a sound.

Behind Pablo, Birdy stirred on the old suitcase. Pablo held his breath so that she would keep sleeping. He kept his eyes focused on the slipping-along shape. It slipped past the flower shop. Past Lula Tattoo. Past Pierre's Goodies—no, it stopped in front of Pierre's picture window. Pablo watched as the shape appeared to grow taller, right there by the window.

Then the shape resolved itself, as if Pablo had been looking at a blurry photo that suddenly regained focus. The shape was a dog. It was *the* dog, the pastry thief, balanced on its hind legs, staring inside the bakery, closed for another few hours until Pierre showed up to start the morning baking.

"Aww," said Pablo. "Poor little guy."

He barely breathed the words—just a whisper of a sound—but Birdy stirred again.

"Poor puppy," whispered Pablo. *"Pobrecito perrito."*

As if the dog could hear them from all that way up, where Pablo was pressing his nose against the window screen, he dropped down to the sidewalk and slunk on his way. Halfway down the block he disappeared into the dark alleyway entrance.

Where did the little *perrito* sleep? There weren't any homes down the alleyway, only a few doors that opened into the backs of shops. Garbage cans. A Dumpster or two. A bunch of trash and broken bricks and other things that Pablo never thought about during the day, because he never went into the alleyway.

Where had the dog come from? The first anyone had seen of him was when he came whipping into the bakery and out again, trailing crumbs of elephant ears and with an enraged Pierre on his heels. But once Lula and Emmanuel realized that the elephant-ear thief was actually a starving little dog, they—and even Pierre, under pressure from Lula—had put out bowls of food for him. He hadn't shown up again, though.

"I guess he's scared of people," Pablo said out loud, as behind him, on the suitcase, Birdy stirred once more.

Then Pablo leaped up, banging his head against the tin edge of the window screen, because an enormous voice suddenly began to shout right there, right in his bedroom.

"GET YOUR MANGY PAWS OFF THERE OR I'LL WHIP YOU WITHIN AN INCH OF YOUR LIFE."

The voice was so loud and mean that Pablo froze, too afraid to turn around. Who was in their apartment? What was he doing in Pablo's bedroom? Who was he talking to? Pablo didn't have paws. Neither did Birdy. These were all the thoughts that ran through his mind in a split second.

Then: *Birdy*.

Birdy couldn't fly. She couldn't squawk. She was small, with only her beak and talons to protect herself against a huge intruder. Pablo whipped around and charged toward the old suitcase, his hands bunched into fists, ready to protect his bird. "Get out!" he screamed at the intruder. "GET OUT!"

But—

—no intruder was there.

There was only Birdy, still asleep despite Pablo's shouting. He scanned the room. No strange man. Nothing. Nothing but his hammock and Emmanuel's old Cuba suitcase with Birdy perched on it, one foot drawn up, deep in sleep.

Dark questions bloomed inside Pablo. He considered waking Emmanuel up to tell him what had just happened. But things were too confusing already, and he didn't want to worry Emmanuel. Had Pablo imagined that awful voice just now, and if so, did that mean he was going crazy? Or—and here he fought back the thought, because hadn't it been proven impossible?—was Birdy, could she, was there any way in the world that . . . no. *No,* he told himself. Birdy was not a Seafarer.

TWENTY

NEXT MORNING PABLO and Birdy were slow in getting to the bakery. Pablo had woken up late to a note from Emmanuel on the counter.

You had some bad dreams last night, mi Pablito. Sleep in and I'll see you and Birdy at Pierre's.

Maybe the awful voice in the middle of the night had been only a bad dream? In the light of day, there in the kitchen with the wooden table and bowl of oranges and limes and smell of coffee, it seemed possible. But Pablo felt tired, and Birdy must too, because her grip on his arm was not as tight as usual.

Outside the sun shone bright. The double-decker bus driver was parked in front of the flower shop, touching up the red paint and gold trim while the flower lady yelled at him to please remove his monstrosity from in front of her shop, that he was not the only one in town who needed to make a living, thank you.

Emmanuel sat at the counter at Pierre's, drinking a café au lait next to Lula, who was sketching out a new tattoo and drinking her mint tea. Pierre was arranging elephant ears and parrot-shaped sugar cookies on trays. The chef and sous-chef from the Parrot Café were huddled at the stand-up table in the far back of the bakery, arguing over their new menu. Shouldn't they add a few new items, parrot-related appetizers or desserts? No, no, no, the old standards were crowd pleasers, and why mess with success?

Mr. Chuckles, Peaches, Rhody, and Sugar Baby came flapping and strutting into the bakery. A small dove cooed her way in after them, close behind Sugar Baby, as if she were trying to fit in, but Peaches and Mr. Chuckles turned in unison and hissed at her and she turned tail and scuttled out.

"Peaches! Mr. Chuckles!" said Pierre. "There will be no bullying in this bakery."

Mr. Chuckles cocked his head and looked Pierre up and down.

"Nice threads," he squawked.

Pierre adjusted his hat and smoothed down his tie. A small sprig of baby's breath poked out of his front pocket. "Really?" he said. One compliment, and Mr. Chuckles was back in Pierre's good graces. Pierre poured himself a large mug of black coffee and clicked on the television. It was Elmira Toledo Special Report time.

Sure enough, there she was in her trench coat, her purple glasses pushed back on her head. She was in the middle of a lecture on the Seafaring Parrot—the special characteristics of the species, an explanation of the properties of sound vibrations—and a list of the current sightings, which she one by one debunked as "piffle." *Piffle* was one of Elmira Toledo's favorite words.

All this was familiar. No one in the bakery paid much attention. It was Elmira Toledo, after all, and this was what she did. Soon she would sign off with her trademark line: "This is Elmira Toledo, reporting on behalf of you and the winds of change, fortune lost or fortune gained."

Except that she didn't. She kept right on going.

"Today we continue our Seafaring Parrot Special Report," said Elmira. "It was nearly ten years ago that three separate fishermen called the Toledo Tip Line with the exact same sighting: a parrotlike bird clinging to a large piece of driftwood."

The camera panned to an oceanlike body of water and then to a driftwood-strewn beach.

"The fishermen were adamant about what they'd seen," said Elmira, "and their descriptions of the bird were virtually identical. That, coupled with the geographical bearings of the fishing boats, led me to the conclusion that if a mythical Seafaring Parrot was indeed spotted *not* flying off the coast of Isla ten years ago, it was under duress and *unable* to fly. Why, you ask? That is the question. My speculation is that some sort of injury prevented the bird from taking to the air."

The camera cut to a photograph of a sad-eyed bird with a splinted wing.

"In which case," finished Elmira, "I have some questions. Did an injured Seafarer wash up on the shore of Isla ten years ago? If so, did it take shelter in the town?"

The camera panned from one end of the beach—their very own beach!—to the other, then zoomed in on Elmira, a stony look on her face.

"And if so, is there still, somewhere in the small town of Isla, way down there in the southernmost part of our country, a living specimen of the most elusive bird in the entire world?"

Everyone in Pierre's was silent, staring at the screen. Elmira's eyes narrowed in her trademark way.

"The winds of change are on their way," she said, emphasizing each word. "And if there is a living Seafarer in existence, then as sure as my name is Elmira Toledo, I intend to find it."

The camera zoomed farther in on her face. She held up a finger, pointed it straight at the lens, and did not blink.

"Isla," she said, "I'm coming for you."

Lula was the first to break the silence.

"Well then," she said. "I guess we've been warned."

Pierre pointed his index finger at Lula's face.

"Lula," he intoned, à la Elmira Toledo, "I'm coming for you."

Emmanuel held an imaginary microphone in front of his mouth. "This is Emmanuel Dominguez, reporting from the town of Isla, where residents are preparing to board up their windows against Tropical Storm Elmira, who is due in any day now."

Lula grabbed the imaginary microphone from Emmanuel.

"And this is Lula St. John, also reporting from Isla, where we all await the arrival of Elmira Toledo in the hopes that she will finally produce an actual, real-life specimen of the genus Seafaringus Parrotus."

Everyone laughed, but it was a nervous laughter. Each of them depended on the tourists for income, but no one liked the crowds, the nosy questions, and the examination of every bird that ordinarily roamed free through the town that went along with a visit from Elmira Toledo. Besides, the focus on the Seafarers was, to use Lula's term, nuts. They of all people would know if there were a Seafarer living among them. Not that they would mind, as long as no one else knew. In fact, it was fascinating to contemplate.

"Think about it," Emmanuel had said. "A bird that can reproduce all the sounds ever made? I could hear my grandmother's voice again."

"And I could hear my family again, back when we all lived together," Lula said. "My mother, my sister, everyone."

"I would have many questions for a Seafarer," Pierre said. "Many, many. *Mais oui.*"

But no one believed that Elmira Toledo was onto anything more than her usual nonsense. They were the ones who had been there when Birdy came floating in to shore, after all. And Birdy had been clinging not to a piece of driftwood, or a white-water raft, or some kind of boogie board, but to a child's blow-up swimming pool. They were the ones who knew what the fishermen calling in their sightings had missed: the parrot-like bird was guarding a baby, a helpless infant cast upon the waves. They were the ones who, when word spread among the townspeople that a Seafaring Parrot was reported to have been spotted floating in to shore, explained that yes, there had been a parrot, and yes, that parrot was now in the care of the townspeople, but no, the parrot was not a Seafaring Parrot. Not at all.

"It's certainly not an African gray," Maria had said, back then. "Nor is it a macaw. Most probably it's a mix of mitred and monk parakeet, lacking the traditional markings of either species. That's my best guess."

When, year after year during press conferences, Maria was asked about the existence of the Seafaring Parrot and whether the reports of sightings could possibly be true, she just smiled.

"I'm a scientist," she would say. "As such I believe only in directly observable scientific data."

This sounded official and impressive, and reporters and townspeople alike would nod and thank Maria for her time. What no one seemed to notice was that she hadn't really answered the question.

It was time to get back to Seafaring Souvenirs, but Pablo couldn't stand the thought of sitting by the cash register ringing up mugs and T-shirts and Painted Parrot shells just now. He scooped Birdy up without even holding out his arm and waiting for her to jump on. Elmira Toledo was as annoying as ever, but today she had left him feeling uneasy.

"No one knows what a Seafaring Parrot actually looks like," said Pablo to Emmanuel, "so what makes her think those old sightings were real?"

"She wants to be famous, probably. The Tip Line is her ticket to fame and fortune."

"Fortune?"

"Sure. Imagine how much money Elmira could get her hands on if she actually had a real-life Seafaring Parrot to parade around."

Making money off the mythical Seafarer was something that Pablo had never considered. Pablo and Emmanuel and lots of others in town, including Lula and Pierre, sold lots of bird souvenirs. But they certainly didn't sell birds themselves. The birds in Isla were free.

TWENTY-ONE

THE LITTLE DOG had grown bolder now that his first two attempts at robbery had gone so well. He was still bedeviled by hunger, but there was a rain puddle near the entrance to the sidewalk, and if he filled his stomach from it, then the hunger pains didn't stab quite as much.

He huddled in the shadows only a couple of feet from the sidewalk. It was so dark in the alleyway compared to the bright sun of the sidewalk that he was nearly invisible. Only someone who knew exactly where he was would be able to find him.

The previous night, the dishwasher at the Parrot Café had emptied the restaurant's trash into the Dumpster outside the café's back door. Oh, the smells. Still-warm arroz con pollo, scraped off plates along with tortillas and beans. It was torment, those smells wafting their way out of the Dumpster and down the alley to where the dog crouched at the rain puddle. When it was fully dark and all motion on the sidewalk ceased, he had trotted down the alleyway to the Dumpster, tantalized by the smell of food.

But the lid was shut tight. And chained.

And it was too high for the dog to get into, even if it had been open. He had propped himself up on his hind feet, scrabbling with his paws just in case there was another way into the Dumpster, but no.

Could he tip it over? Garbage cans were tippable. Maybe Dumpsters were the same. He scrabbled again, throwing his scrawny weight behind his paws.

No.

The Dumpster was built to last. It was solid and heavy and its lid was closed and all in all it was a terrible situation. The dog had given up and made his way back to the rain puddle. There was only so much puddle a dog could drink before either his stomach twisted up with pain or the puddle dried up.

Or both, which was the case for the dog.

Now, though, it was the next day. The dog's nose once more filled with the familiar smell of cinnamon and sugar and butter. Irresistible. He could almost taste those elephant ears.

Closer and closer he crept to the sunshine.

Could he?

Would—

—Oh no. There was the bird again, clinging to the boy. She turned her eyes to the alleyway just as they passed by, trailed by that pack of grumbling birds.

Silent bird and silent dog, eyes locked. But then screams and cries and laughter and songs filled the dog's head. The dog had endured so much suffering and deprivation in his young life that his senses were keen, much keener than the placid leashed dogs of Isla. But even so, he had never been able to hear the sounds that were trapped inside another creature's head. He retreated immediately, back into the shadows, trying to get away from all that noise. All that good noise, all that bad noise, all that noise, noise, endless noise. He would have fled if there were any place to run where the people beyond the alleyway wouldn't see him and try to chase him down.

If he were that bird, he would fly away. Fly as fast as he could. Fly and fly and fly, if only to outfly all that noise.

TWENTY-TWO

THAT NIGHT PABLO woke up to find no sleeping-Birdy-shadow on the Cuba suitcase. She wasn't silhouetted against the window screen either. He swung himself out of his hammock and went looking for her. It was a clear night and the grotesque was visible across the street, the swallows' mud nests dark and still underneath the stone ledge.

The kitchen was dark and quiet. Pablo peeked into Emmanuel's bedroom, where he was curled up and asleep under his blanket. No Birdy there.

No sign of her in the living room either. Back to his bedroom he went. He turned around in the dim moonlight, searching.

"Birdy?" he whispered, then louder, "Birdy?"

No fluttering of wings or *click-click* of talons in response. Pablo went over to the window and peered out into the moonlit night, across the chasm of darkness to where the grotesque crouched on its stone ledge. The screen was pushed up a few inches from the other night, when he had spied the little dog slinking down the sidewalk. The steel cable gleamed all the way across to the grotesque's ledge. It was a windless night, calm and clear and silent, so why was the cable moving? He followed its shimmying length with his eyes . . . and then he saw the dark shadow halfway across. Birdy!

She was out there! She had made her way out the window, jumped off the ledge and onto the cable, and now she was on her way to . . . where? The grotesque? It didn't matter.

Pablo's mind worked frantically.

She couldn't fly. She could fall at any moment, tumble through the air like the baby sparrows who were too small to fly. He reached out and gripped the steel cable with his hands, trying to haul it and Birdy back through the air to his side. The cable stopped trembling. The dark shadow of Birdy stopped inching out into space and stayed still. Below her, the giant silk-screened parrot hung motionless, its eyes burning in the moonlight.

"Please, Birdy," Pablo said. Softly, so as not to startle her and cause her to fall. "Please come back."

It was as if the air itself were holding its breath, so still and soundless was it outside. Pablo waited, both hands on the cable. Across the way, the grotesque was also motionless. Its eyes, cavelike in the night, were unreadable.

"Please, Birdy."

And finally, Birdy turned around. She began to slide her feet one after the other back along the cable toward Pablo. She inched her way along,

closer, closer, closer, until the gap between them was closed, and she was on the window ledge. Then his hands were around her and he eased her back inside, into the room, which suddenly felt stuffy and airless after the cool outdoor air.

Pablo closed the window screen. Outside, the cable was dark and still. It had felt alive under his fingers, glittering in the moonlight, when Birdy inched along it toward the grotesque.

"Birdy," Pablo said. She drooped against his chest. "Birdy, what were you doing?"

No answer.

"You could have fallen," he said. "You could have fallen all that way down, and I wouldn't even have known."

No answer.

"What if I woke up and you were just . . . gone? And I had no idea where you were?"

No answer.

"You didn't even wake me up. You didn't tell me where you were going. You didn't say goodbye."

That got her attention. She lifted her head and looked at him. He didn't mean to, but he started to cry.

"You can't leave me, Birdy. Please don't leave me."

Now she pushed back against him and cocked her head. She swatted him with her wing, gently, and then she folded both wings around him and buried her head in the crook of his neck. Pablo didn't know what to do. Nothing like this had ever happened before. Birdy had never left his side.

Last night, the horrible voice in his room. Tonight, Birdy halfway across the street, only the steel cable to keep her from falling to her death. What was happening? The image of Darren Mandible, dipping and swirling and talking about the winds of change, popped into his mind.

He felt for his necklace under his T-shirt. *Dios me bendiga.*

Maybe he should tell Emmanuel. Or Maria. But they wouldn't know what to do either, would they? Besides, Pablo was the one who knew Birdy best. He tucked her back against his blanket, then went to the window and pressed his head against the closed screen and looked across at the grotesque at the other end of the cable. He pictured Birdy inching out on the cable, her wings slightly lifted. *What if she had fallen?*

"She didn't," he said out loud. "She didn't fall. Stop thinking about it."

But what about all the times he and Birdy had stood together at this window, watching the baby birds across the way learn to fly? Watching them fling themselves out of their mud nests right onto the thin air? She had watched them so closely, her eyes following their awkward, tumbling flights.

Pablo thought of the questions Maria had asked him about Birdy. Had she ever flown, had she ever plucked out her feathers, had she ever talked? He had answered no to the first two questions, and he had told Maria about the muttered whisper when Birdy was asleep. He had told her about the *pobrecito Pablo,* but he had not told her about the man's loud voice in his room. Then again, how did he know that Birdy had been the one to yell those awful words? He could imagine what Maria would say if he told her he'd found Birdy out on the cable.

Did she actually fly, though? Maria would say, and he would have to say, *No.*

There was a nudge at his shoulder. Birdy had fluttered up to stand next to him. Pablo put his arm around her, just in case she got any ideas, and they pressed their heads against the screen and looked down. The block was dark and quiet as it always was in the night.

Not entirely, though. Something was moving, down there in the darkness. Was it the little dog out again, lured by the memory of elephant ears?

No. Not the dog. Too small to be the dog. Pablo squinted and waited for his eyes to come into focus. Something was moving down there, in the middle of the street. Not just one something but several. The Committee! They were awake and gathered in the middle of the empty street, as if they were having a meeting. Next to him, Birdy shifted from foot to foot and half raised her wings.

They all looked up, right then, as if they had heard the faint click of her talons on the window-sill. Their small bird faces were illuminated in the moonlight. They froze at the sight of Pablo in the window next to Birdy. But it was too late. He had seen them.

"Committee!" Pablo called. "What are you doing down there?"

Silence. Even from four flights up, Pablo could see how Peaches and Sugar Baby and Mr. Chuckles turned to one another, as if they'd been caught and were trying to come up with some kind of answer. Not so with Rhody.

Cock-a-doodle-doooooooo.

None of the others made a sound. But there they were, gathered in the street. The little dog the other night, now the Committee. And Birdy, risking her life out there on the cable. What was happening? Pablo again pictured Darren Mandible as he had been the other day, all excited about the possibility of winds of change. About fortune lost and fortune gained.

Cock-a-doodle-dooooooooooo.

Far below, Rhody was at it again.

TWENTY-THREE

THE DOG SLEPT fitfully. It was pitch black in the alley, with only a few stars visible above the buildings that rose up on either side of him. He was curled up next to the Dumpster. Hours had gone by since the dishwasher had emptied that night's garbage into the Dumpster and closed the lid, but the delicious food smells still emanated from it.

The smells infiltrated the dog's dreams. So had the smells from the small bowls of food the tattoo lady and the elephant-ear man set out for him, until a pudgy village dog had gone and gobbled them both up when the boy holding its leash had been distracted. Now the little dog was back to square one. In his dreams, which were always about food, he was back in the house he'd escaped from, and the man was cooking himself something to eat.

A steak. Potatoes. Cornbread. Butter.

The dog stood in the far corner of the kitchen, not moving. He made no sound. He was waiting. There was a chance that the man would, when he was finished eating, put his plate on the floor. If he did, that was the signal to inch forward, in silence, and eat from the man's plate. If the man didn't put the plate on the floor, though, that was the signal that the dog would get no food that night.

The only way the plate would be put on the floor was if the dog was perfectly quiet. Soundless. Unmoving.

The man's fork scraped on the plate. His knife sawed through the meat. He brought the fork to his mouth and lowered it. Up with the fork, down. Up. Down.

Only the dog's eyes moved. He held himself perfectly still.

The man finished his dinner. He got up and put the plate in the sink without a word to the dog.

No food that night.

In the dog's sleep, his hind legs twitched and his front legs moved in unison. The plate in the sink smelled of food. Food, food, food. Then the distant crowing of a rooster pierced his dream.

Cock-a-doodle-doooooo.

TWENTY-FOUR

THE NEXT NIGHT Pablo sat at the kitchen table painting more tiny parrots. It was hard to keep up with them, they sold so fast. Especially the ones of Peaches, who looked quite a bit more noble, majestic even, in Pablo's paintings than she did in real life. Plus, no one could hear her squawking.

Emmanuel was making black beans and rice and fried plantains, which he called the national dish of Cuba. Emmanuel loved Cuban food, and he had raised Pablo to love it too. Which he did, even though, if given the choice, Pablo would still choose cheese quesadillas.

Birdy was restless, hopping from the table to the floor, fluttering up to the living room window and back down again. Pablo was restless too, but only on the inside. He concentrated on guiding the minuscule paintbrush up and down the faint outline of Peaches that he had penciled onto the smooth interior of the shell. His eyes kept going to Birdy. Now she was up on the windowsill again, her wings lifted ever so slightly, so that her blue-green under-feathers gleamed iridescent in the lamplight.

"Emmanuel?"

"Hmm?"

Pablo wanted to talk to him about Birdy—it was on the tip of his tongue to bring it up—but what would he tell him? That he'd found her on the cable in the middle of the night? That sometimes—often, these days—she whispered in her sleep? And maybe even said actual words? Loud words, if in fact she was the one who had spoken in the man's voice the other night. Emmanuel was bent over the cutting board, his knife moving swiftly on the plantains. Rice and black beans, each in covered pots, simmered on the back burners. The smell began to fill the room. Pablo's mouth watered, and he concentrated on painting the curve of Peaches's considerable wingspan.

Now was not the time to talk to Emmanuel about Birdy. It would just make everything more complicated than it already was.

"You have a question, *mi Pablito*?"

"Yeah. Is it okay if I put on some music?"

Emmanuel looked up and smiled. "Sure, as long as it's you know who."

Which meant the Buena Vista Social Club. Emmanuel's favorite music. He said it reminded him of Old Cuba, which was where his family had come from when he was a little boy.

"We're a nation of immigrants," he had told Pablo many times. "Isla especially. Almost everyone who lives in this country came from somewhere else. Like my family from Cuba, and Lula's from Haiti. Pierre too. He came from Saskatchewan, Canada, even though he tries to pretend it was France instead."

This conversation usually happened around the time of Pablo's non-birthday. Pablo was pretty sure that Emmanuel was trying to make him feel better, because he, too, had come from somewhere else. It didn't make him feel better, though. Emmanuel's parents had passed away, but Emmanuel knew who they were and where his whole family had come from. He knew his own story. Whereas Pablo didn't.

It's not the same, he wanted to say whenever Emmanuel brought it up, but he had always kept quiet. But tonight he had questions that wouldn't go away.

"Emmanuel, why did your family leave Cuba?" he asked.

"For the same reason that most people leave their home, Pablito," Emmanuel said. "To make a new life somewhere."

"But why?" Pablo persisted. "Why would anyone want to leave their home?"

Emmanuel stirred the beans. Around and around and around went the spoon. It took him a long time to answer.

"It's not always a question of want, my boy. Countries can be like families. Sometimes they argue with other countries, or the people in one country argue with each other. Things turn bad. Life can feel impossible, whether because there's no way to make a living or there's war or, for whatever reason, you don't feel free. Things changed in Cuba a long time ago—the government changed—and my parents were afraid."

He was still stirring the beans, but he looked up at Pablo and sighed. "Life was hard for them there, and it was hard for them here, too," he said. "Hard for a long time. It is not easy to leave your country, your language, everything you know."

"Emmanuel?"

"Yes?"

"Do you think that's what happened to me?"

Awful though it was to contemplate, the idea of his original family trying to escape with him was better than the thought that he had been a horrible baby sent out to sea in a swimming pool. But Emmanuel lifted his shoulders and shook his head. "I don't know, Pablo. I wish, for your sake, that I did."

Emmanuel looked sad just then, so sad that Pablo felt bad for asking his questions. After all, he had a family, didn't he? He had Emmanuel, and he had Birdy. He had his friends, Oswaldo especially, and he had Lula and Pierre, who were like family. Just think of the poor little thieving dog, who from the scrawny, matted look of him had no one at all.

"I wonder where the *perrito* sleeps at night," said Emmanuel, as if he could read Pablo's mind. He dropped the plantains into the hot frying pan, laced his fingers together behind his head, stretched, and yawned. "I wish I knew if it's him who eats the food we leave out for him. I hope so. Poor little pup."

"I don't want him to be hungry," said Pablo.

"He'd probably like some black beans and rice about now," said Emmanuel. "I know I would."

Pablo lifted the needle on the arm of the old record player and placed it down on the Buena Vista Social Club record that was always in place. Emmanuel turned the burner to low and held out his arms to Birdy, who looked away.

"Dance with me, Birdita?"

She acted as though she hadn't heard him.

"Fine," said Emmanuel. "Ignore me. You wouldn't be the first lady to refuse a dance with Emmanuel."

"Liar," said Pablo, and Emmanuel smiled. All the ladies, and some of the men, wanted to dance with Emmanuel. It had been that way as long as Pablo could remember. But Emmanuel always said he was happy just the way he was, with Pablo and Birdy and lots of T-shirts to design and a store to run.

"If you could dance with anyone in the world, who would you dance with, Emmanuel?"

"Oh, *mi Pablito*, good question."

"Lula? Maria? Elmira Toledo?"

"My mother," Emmanuel said. "That's who I'd dance with. I wish you'd known her, Pablo. Oh, what a dancer she was."

He circled slowly around the kitchen, his arms around an imaginary partner.

"So, my boy," he said mid-twirl. "There's something else I've been wanting to talk to you about. It has to do with your birthday."

"It's not even my real birthday."

Pablo looked up from his painting in surprise. Had he actually said that? No! He hadn't! He hadn't said anything. Emmanuel had stopped dancing and looked as surprised as Pablo felt.

"Pablito?" Emmanuel said, but Pablo shook his head. They both turned and looked at Birdy, who was standing on the windowsill with lifted wings. She strained her head forward and opened her beak. Pablo heard his own voice again, even though that couldn't be, because his mouth was shut tight.

"It's not even my real birthday," said Birdy again, in Pablo's voice. "Right?"

Emmanuel turned from Birdy to Pablo and back again. Confusion spread across his face.

"Pablo?" he said. "I could've sworn that—"

"It was me," said Pablo, lying instantly. "I've been practicing ventriloquism. I'm doing good, aren't I?"

His voice sounded false even to his own ears. He hated to lie. But he just kept sitting there at the table, guiding the tiny brush around the penciled lines of Peaches's profile, not saying anything else, not meeting Emmanuel's eyes, and after a while Emmanuel sat down at the table.

"Pablito," he said, "look at me."

Pablo kept his eyes on the shell. Peaches was almost finished. One more stroke of black, to outline her eye—Pablo always emphasized the parrots' eyes in his painted shells—and then he could paint *African gray* on the rim of the shell and set her aside.

"Pablito."

No. If Pablo looked up at Emmanuel now, he would start to cry. And if he cried, then who knew what might come out? His non-birthday, the fact that he didn't have any photos of people who looked like him, the sad thought that his original parents had lived in fear and left their country. And Birdy, too. The awful words she had spoken in her sleep the other night. The fact that he had found her out on the cable, heading toward the grotesque. No, there were too many troubling things swirling around in his brain, and he wasn't ready to talk about any of them. He kept his eyes on his work instead.

"Something is on your mind, *mi Pablito,*" Emmanuel said. "On mine, too."

"I don't want to talk about it."

After a while Emmanuel got up and came around behind Pablo and put his hands on Pablo's shoulders.

"When you're ready, then."

He leaned down and kissed the top of Pablo's head, and then he went back to the stove.

TWENTY-FIVE

ON THE TELEVISION screen at Pierre's the next day, Darren Mandible was so excited at what he termed "the high probability" of the winds of change that he could not stop smiling. He was wearing what Lula referred to as his disco pants, because they were white and stretchy. This was a good thing, because when Darren was excited about the weather, he almost danced around the weather map. His pointer swept from side to side on the map, and every sentence ended with an exclamation mark.

"Exciting new wind developments just off-shore of the picturesque island town of Isla!"

Darren placed a wind magnet right over Isla on his weather map—*smack*—then turned back to the camera and did a little hop.

"For the first time since I can recall, weather hounds, the Isla winds are beginning to blow not onshore, but *away*! AWAY! Which can portend only one thing!"

He stabbed the pointer toward the camera and nodded furiously. His ponytail flapped back and forth.

"Winds of change! Fortune lost, fortune gained!"

"I have yet to see a fortune of any kind," said Lula, "let alone lose one."

"And here is my colleague Elmira Toledo with the latest! Elmira?"

Elmira was dressed in a sky-blue trench coat today, her purple glasses dangling from her non-microphone fingers.

"Darren," said Elmira. "Exciting developments to be sure. Who among us *isn't* interested in the existence of the Seafarer?"

"A few of us," said Lula.

"More than a few of us," said Pierre.

The camera cut from Elmira to a white laboratory, where a large cage was set up in the corner. Scientific-looking people, lots of them, stood next to the cage holding clipboards. They were unsmiling. The camera cut back to Elmira, who was also unsmiling. Then again, Elmira was always unsmiling.

"Proactive preparation on the part of our panel of experts from the avian scientific community has resulted in a new laboratory," she said, "created with the express purpose of studying the Seafaring Parrot, once a specimen is available for research."

The experts themselves, interviewed in turn, were divided on the existence of the Seafaring Parrot, given that the legend had held sway over the public mind for a long time. That fact alone raised suspicions in the minds of some of the scientists.

"Certainly, sound lasts longer than we perceive it," said one. "But we humans hear it only as it happens, just like the rest of the animal world. Why would one bird out of the thousands of bird species in the world be able to hear all sound, at any time? It doesn't make sense."

Others agreed. Science was about making sense, they said, and scientific principle held that the most obvious explanation was usually the correct explanation.

"Which leads us to human nature," said another. "Human beings are creatures of longing. They want to believe that the voices of their loved ones are still there, still available to them. Whether it's true or not is a different matter entirely."

Most of the experts believed that the legend of the Seafaring Parrot was just that: legend. There was simply no scientific basis to back up that legend, they claimed. But Elmira Toledo's response was equally simple.

"That is only because none have been captured," she said. "Until we have a Seafarer in captivity and are able to study it, these questions will remain. That is why it is essential to find one and confine it in an enclosed space where we can study it."

The camera panned around the bright white laboratory. The cage was empty, save for a water bottle and a feeder attached to the side, a wooden perch, and what looked to be a bank of microphones arrayed along the top and sides. Electronic screens with wiggling colored bars were arrayed on the other side of the lab.

Pierre and Lula and Emmanuel and Pablo and Maria frowned.

"Wouldn't life in a cage kill a Seafaring Parrot?" said Pierre.

"According to legend, yes," said Maria. "Supposedly they die in captivity."

"Imagine if we had a Seafarer in custody," Elmira said, as if she could hear them. "Imagine if this mythical bird can in fact call forth the voices of the past. Imagine the questions of the past that could be laid to rest. Imagine the history that could be set straight."

Elmira tilted her head and leaned into the camera.

"What are the voices that *you*, viewers, would call forth if you could?" she said. "Think about it. Hallowed voices from the past, brought to historical life again, through the singular abilities of the Seafaring Parrot."

"She stole that question from my public art project!" said Lula. "Plagiarism! Copyright infringement! Question thief!"

"She's really putting her all into it this year," Pierre said. "Ratings must be down."

"Makes my blood boil," said Lula. "But it's still a good question. Whose voice *would* you bring back, if you could?"

"Someone important, of course," said Pierre. "Someone essential to the course of human history. Someone, let's see, someone . . ."

"Oh, be honest," said Lula. "Tell the truth. Don't be like all the tourists who just write down famous people."

"My grandfather, then. I would give almost

anything to hear my grandfather's voice just one more time. He used to sing 'Happy Birthday' to me every year." Pierre's eyes looked bright.

"Good choice," said Lula. "As for me, I would bring back the voice of my sister as a baby."

"I thought you and your sister weren't speaking anymore," said Pierre. "Didn't you have a big fight years ago?"

"We did."

"What was it about?"

She shook her head. "Something stupid. I don't even remember."

"Have you tried to call her?"

"Once. She hung up on me. But sometimes I think about her, the way we were when we were little. How she would laugh and laugh."

Pablo looked over at Birdy. She was standing on a chair, pecking at a plate of chopped mango. She didn't meet his eyes. She appeared to be completely focused on the mango. But Pablo was pretty sure she hadn't missed a single word of the conversation.

"How about you, Emmanuel?" Lula said. "Whose voice would you bring back?"

Emmanuel looked down at his hands, then over at Pablo. His eyes were dark and sad.

"Come on," said Pierre. "Tell us."

But Emmanuel just shook his head. And no one asked Pablo.

TWENTY-SIX

DOWN ON THE floor, Peaches and Sugar Baby were fighting over the same shred of coconut. Rhody had lost interest and wandered back outside, while Mr. Chuckles was laughing quietly to himself—"hahahahaha"—in the corner. Maria had left to open the clinic. Two overheated tourists sat at a table in the back, fanning themselves with plastic fold-up Seafarer fans and bickering about how to spend the rest of the day. Just then there came a commotion outside the bakery. The skittering of paws on the sidewalk, the flashing of a lopsided tail, and the dog—the dog!—tore in, followed by Rhody in hot pursuit.

"Not again!" shouted Pierre, as the dog raced behind the counter, leaped up, and snatched an elephant ear. "I forbid this! Drop that pastry!"

"Cock-a-doodle-doo!"

"HAHAHAHAHA!"

"Holy crud!" said Lula. "That dog does not give up!"

The dog had made it halfway back to the door, crumbs spewing from his mouth, lopsided tail waving wildly, when a voice, a man's voice, began shouting.

"YOU DESPICABLE CREATURE. YOU UGLY, NO-GOOD DOG."

Instantly, the dog skidded to a near halt and lowered himself onto his belly. He began to crawl toward the door. Fear rose from every trembling inch of him. The voice thundered down again.

"WORTHLESS MUTT."

The dog's eyes rolled with fear. Pablo's heart

pounded in his chest. He looked around for the man, the awful man who must belong to the awful voice. But there was no one in the bakery but Pablo and Lula and Pierre and Emmanuel and the bickering tourists. And they all were staring at Birdy, who was standing on the chair with her wings raised.

"It's okay," Pablo said. "It's okay." He knelt on the floor next to the dog, who was still on his belly, still trembling. There was silence behind them. Pablo was afraid to turn his head. He put one hand on the dog's side to soothe him. Sharp ribs felt as if they were poking right through the dog's long, matted fur.

"Poor guy," said Pablo.

"Pobrecito," said a woman's voice. *"Pobrecito."*

Pablo kept his hand on the dog's trembling side and swiveled around to see Emmanuel, Lula, Pierre, and the tourists now gaping at Birdy. She was shifting from foot to foot. She opened her beak and *"Pobrecito,"* she said again. There could be no denying that it was Birdy. Birdy, speaking in a woman's soft, sad voice. She hid her head in her feathers, which were all ruffled up as if she'd been out in a strong wind. But the voice came again, muffled and full of sorrow. It was the same voice that Pablo had heard in the middle of the night.

Pobrecito.

"Birdy?" said Lula.

Birdy raised her head and looked at Lula, then ducked back into her feathers. The others had still not said a word. Their argument forgotten, the bickering tourists were now taking photo after photo, turning their cell phones this way and that and murmuring to each other. Pablo distinctly heard the words *Toledo Tip Line* before they abruptly turned and slipped out the door. Emmanuel broke the silence.

"Birdy?" he said, his voice full of astonishment. "Birdy, *mi Birdita, eres un*"—here his voice turned to a whisper—*"Seafarer?"*

At the word *Seafarer*, whispered though it was, Pablo held his breath. Birdy was on the chair, huddled into herself with an air of misery. Tears were running down Lula's cheeks, while awe spread across Pierre's face. Emmanuel's eyes were filled with wonder.

"Mon dieu," Pierre whispered. "All this time. All these years."

"It's a miracle," Emmanuel said.

Lula tried to say something, but her voice was choked with tears. She got down on her knees and clasped her hands together and bowed her head. And Pablo? All Pablo could think of was getting to Birdy. Picking her up off that chair where she kept shifting from foot to foot, the chair where she stood alone, the chair where anyone who looked into the bakery could see her. So many thoughts rushed through his mind—Birdy asleep on the Cuba suitcase next to his hammock while the man's voice shouted in anger about a dog, Birdy silent while the Committee gabbled and squawked around her, Birdy spreading her wings while Pablo almost-flew her down the beach—but one thought rose up bigger than all the others, which was that Birdy needed him. He had to get to her.

Pablo sat up, but as he started to stand the dog heaved himself up, toenails clicking on the tile floor. His lopsided tail tucked itself down the way that Birdy had tucked her head into her feathers, and he shoved his head into Pablo's neck as if he was trying to hide himself. Trying to tell him to stay, to please not leave. Pablo put an arm around him and hugged him close, but the dog didn't stop trembling.

"It's a miracle," Emmanuel said again.

"It is," Lula agreed, drying her tears. "Birdy can talk—Birdy can *talk.*" Wonder spread across her face, but then she shook her head as if trying to focus. "It's a miracle that could become a tragedy. Are the rest of you thinking what I'm thinking?"

"Toledo?" Pierre said.

"The Tip Line?" Emmanuel said.

Lula nodded. "Elmira and her henchmen are on their way, and the only thing they care about is finding a Seafarer. We have to help Birdy."

On the chair, Birdy shifted her weight. She looked miserable, as miserable as the dog on the floor.

"There's no one here," Pablo whispered into the dog's ear. "The mean man is gone. He was never here at all."

But as he said it, he knew that wasn't quite true. In a way, the mean man *had* been there. His voice had anyway. Then another voice came back to him: Elmira's. *Until we have a Seafarer in captivity* . . .

"Stay here," Pablo whispered to the dog. "I have to go, but you're safe here."

Birdy wasn't, though. Pablo got to his feet, walked to the chair, and held out his arm to his bird.

A few others were down on the beach—a tattooed father carrying a baby, a woman collecting sand dollars—but not many. Pablo went to the far end, where a disintegrating oyster boat leaned against some rocks. He sat down in the hull so that he and Birdy wouldn't be visible to anyone. She perched there on the bottom of the boat.

Pablo felt for his necklace and closed his fingers around it. He turned it over and over, until the leather cord was tight around his neck. Had his mother given it to him? Could his mother possibly be the woman with the soft, sad voice? *Pobrecito Pablo.*

Maybe he hadn't been a horrid baby, screaming all the time so that whoever his parents had been, they were happy to see him go. Maybe he'd had parents who loved him. Who wanted him. Who would never have let him go unless they had to. And when they had to, maybe they had put him in the only thing they had at hand, the only thing that might keep him alive, that might give him a chance to survive. Didn't that make more sense than the other stories?

But no one ever talked about *that* possibility. Pirate baby, precocious baby, emissary from a forgotten world. Those were just stories, made up for fun. But they weren't fun anymore.

It was a warm morning, but Pablo shivered. Next to him, Birdy was shifting from foot to foot. She ducked her head under her feathers as if she knew what he was thinking, and she didn't want to think about it.

"Birdy," he said, "I know you can hear me. So I'm just going to talk."

Once he said that, though, he went quiet. The thing he had wondered about for so long, the question he had asked Maria about, was clear. She had always said that no one knew what exactly a Seafaring Parrot looked like.

But now, Pablo did.

Seafaring Parrots were lavender, with underfeathers of iridescent blue-green. Medium height, medium build. Dark eyes. Did every Seafarer look like Birdy? If they did, then the far reaches of the ocean skies must be beautiful with birds.

"Birdy?" he said. "What's it like, to hear everything, forever?"

He had tried to imagine it before, and now he

tried again. Just think of knowing the happiest things that everyone in the world had ever said. The most loving things. The kindest. It would be beautiful, but it would also be overwhelming. Then he imagined just the opposite. What if you held, inside your own head, the saddest things said by every person in the entire world?

"Can you tell me?" he said.

She tilted her head and looked at him for a minute, as if she were thinking. Then she opened her beak and sound came pouring forth. Voices in languages familiar—English and Spanish—and entirely unfamiliar, both human and animal, singing and crying and calling and whispering. The natural world, leaves in the wind, the crack of thunder, rain, first a patter, then a deluge, the howl of what might be a tornado. Pablo's head filled with noise, a cacophony of it. A man's voice shouting in anger, a child's shriek of fear, a woman's voice calling something over and over, the *crack* of a tree falling, the groan of wood pulling apart.

Oh no.

This was all too much. Instinctively he closed his eyes and put his hands over his ears to block it out, but the noise was everywhere. It was more than he could bear. More than anyone could bear. Maybe Maria was right. Maybe it was better not to know. He felt a nudge on his shoulder and opened his eyes. Birdy, her eyes focused and intent. She opened her beak again, but this time there was only one voice, soft and sweet, the same voice as the *pobrecito Pablo* voice. She was singing a song with a slow lilt, a song that repeated itself. A lullaby, maybe.

"Who is that, Birdy?"

She didn't answer him. She just kept singing, the same little song, over and over.

"Is that . . . my mother?"

No answer.

"Please, Birdy. You have to know who it is. Please tell me."

She stopped singing and ducked her head into her feathers, burrowing. Was she trying to hide? But if she was a Seafarer, why *didn't* she tell him? And why didn't she fly? Confusion filled him. And not just confusion but frustration. None of this made sense.

"Birdy, if you're a Seafarer, then why don't you fly?"

She just kept looking at him.

"You're supposed to, aren't you?" he said. "I mean, everyone says that Seafarers *have* to fly, or they'll"—the word was *die* but he couldn't stand to say it—"be sad and . . . and . . . unhappy."

At that, she burrowed her head deeper. "Stop hiding," he said. "We have to figure this out. I don't know why you won't just talk to me. And I don't know what to do. I don't know how to help."

But she wasn't trying to hide this time. When she untucked her head, there was something in her beak.

"What is that?" said Pablo, and she extended her head so that he could see. A feather. She was holding it out to him. He took the feather—long and blue-green and so light it was like holding air in his hand—and brought it to his nose. It smelled of her: warm and dusty, with the scent of mangoes. Pablo put both hands around her and lifted her to his chest. Maria's warning, that plucked feathers were a sign of distress, hung in his mind.

"All right, Birdy-bird," he said. "It's going to be okay."

He kept both hands around her, gently, all the way back from the beach, all the way to Maria's Critter Clinic.

TWENTY-SEVEN

FEAR STILL PRICKLED down the dog's back as he hunched up next to the outside wall of the bakery. When the boy and the bird left, he had waited until a little strength came back to him, then slunk outside, away from the people who were now talking intently. It was a good time to sneak out, before their attention returned to him. Before they trapped him and locked him up for stealing, or before the man found him. It was a world full of danger. The dog looked up the street and then down.

Hadn't he gotten away from the man?

Far away?

The sound of his voice had brought the dog right back to the house on the edge of the woods, the house where the man yelled and yelled. The house where he took off his belt and came after the dog, slapping it against his palm and advancing step by step. Step by step by step, until the dog had huddled himself as far back in the farthest back room as he could. Until there was nowhere else to go.

YOU WORTHLESS MUTT.

Those words. The feel of them in his ears.

The feel of the belt on his back and legs and paws and head.

The ears and the paws hurt the worst.

There were other houses next to the house where the man yelled at the dog and beat the dog. When he managed to sneak up on the bed and lean his front paws on the window, the dog could see them. Lights glowed in their kitchens and living rooms, upstairs in their bedrooms.

There were people in those houses. But no one ever came to knock at the house where the man yelled at the dog, where he beat the dog and fed him only when he felt like it and not when the dog was hungry. Which was all the time.

Maybe the neighbors were afraid of the man too. Or maybe they didn't know there was a dog in the house.

The dog had lived in fear for weeks, months, close to a year. He had lived without enough food or clean water. He had lived without love. But he had not ever, even though he came very close, lived without hope. Just a shred of hope. And then came the night when the man didn't return to the house.

The dog waited many hours before he snuck onto the bed again, in the darkness, and put his front paws up on the window. Other houses were lit. He could see people moving in them behind the windows. In one, a family sat around a table eating. The dog took a deep breath. Yes, they were eating: bread and butter and carrots and stew. He could smell it all. Saliva spiraled down from his mouth. He jumped off the bed and trotted into the kitchen. He nosed at the closet where the man kept the bag of food he sometimes doled out to the dog. With one paw, he nudged the door open. But the bag was empty.

No food.

The dog's stomach growled. He bent to the water bowl. That was empty too, so he went to the bathroom and gulped water out of the toilet.

Then he went to the back door, and then the front door, sniffing deeply at the seams in each door, hoping to scent the man's car coming down the road. He could usually smell it from far off.

But not tonight.

Back and forth from door to door he trotted, following the well-worn path in the carpet. This was a trek he had made many times. The man had sworn at him and kicked him for wearing out the carpet, but the dog didn't know why he was being yelled at or kicked. He didn't know he was wearing a path in the carpet. All he knew was that he was waiting for the man to come home, because even if that meant yelling and beating, it also meant that there might be food.

And if the dog had never had affection, he had also never, ever had enough food.

It was on the tenth, or the hundredth, or maybe the thousandth, trip from the front door to the back door that the dog heard a creak. Was the man home? Had he somehow missed the smell and the sound of the car? He hunched back against the wall, waiting for the stomp and tromp and flicking on of light. But there was nothing, just a slight creak of the back door.

That was when the dog noticed that the door was not entirely closed. He nudged it with his paw, the same way he nudged the closet door.

It opened.

The dog made his decision instantly. He did not think. He did not hesitate. What he did was take off, straight into the woods. And he kept moving, for days, maybe weeks, until he came to Isla, the town of elephant ears and roaming birds, and the alley where he had taken refuge.

TWENTY-EIGHT

PABLO CRADLED BIRDY to his chest and pushed open the door to the clinic with his foot. Maria was just coming out of the back room with her clipboard. In her white coat she looked for a moment like one of the unsmiling scientists in the white laboratory on the television screen, waiting for a live specimen of the mythical Seafaring Parrot.

Then she smiled, and Pablo's heart jumped in relief.

"Pablo?" she said. "Are you and Birdy okay?"

Pablo shook his head and glanced around the waiting room. No one was there but one of the alpacas on a leash. The leash was wound around the ficus tree in the corner and the alpaca, who was munching on a flake of hay, seemed perfectly happy. He eyed Pablo and Birdy, blinked once, and then went back to the hay.

"Sit down," said Maria. She sat down on the orange couch and Pablo, still clutching Birdy, sat down next to her. "What's going on? Tell me."

At first Pablo couldn't speak. Birdy was quiet against his chest. She had tucked her head down into her feathers again. She didn't push her beak into the crook of his neck, the way she usually did.

"She's talking," Pablo blurted.

"Who's talking?"

"Birdy."

Then it all came out: the words about his birthday, spoken in his own voice last night, this morning's horrible words shouted in the bakery, and how everyone sitting there had been shocked into silence. How the pastry-thief dog had been instantly terrified, almost unable to move, huddled on his belly on the floor. How Pablo had tried to soothe him and felt the sharpness of his ribs underneath all that dirty, tangled fur. How Birdy had tried to hide herself under her own feathers. And all the sounds that had come pouring out of her when he'd asked her about her life, about what it was like to hear everything forever.

"And Darren Mandible was talking about the winds of change, and how they're coming again, but this time they're weird, because they're going to blow *offshore,* not onshore, and there are a whole bunch of scientists in a laboratory with a cage and they have clipboards, like yours"—here he jutted his chin at Maria's clipboard—"except that your clipboard is good and theirs aren't, and they're waiting for a Seafaring Parrot to be captured so they can put it in the cage and study it, and . . . and . . . and . . ."

"And you're worried that Birdy is . . ."

"A Seafarer! Yes!"

At that, Birdy untucked her head from her

feathers. She pushed off from Pablo's chest, which made him clutch her tighter. She opened her beak and strained her head back, but made no sound. Maria put one hand on Birdy's back, stroking her feathers, and the other on Pablo's shoulder.

"And there were two tourists in the bakery and they were taking a bunch of photos and I heard them say 'Tip Line' and if Elmira Toledo finds Birdy, she'll lock her up!"

Birdy's talons dug into his arms. Now she started pecking against his T-shirt. Now she was pecking at his necklace. *Clink. Clink.* He couldn't cover it up because both hands were occupied, trying to keep her still. Maria was silent.

"Didn't you hear me?" Pablo was being rude but he didn't care. "They'll lock her up in a cage. And Seafarers die if they're locked up in cages. Seafarers have to fly."

Maria's hand was still on his shoulder. She was petting Birdy like a kitten, tiny little strokes down her back. But Birdy was still struggling, digging her talons into Pablo's T-shirt.

"They have to *fly*," Pablo said again.

"Birdy doesn't fly, though."

"But she wants to. I found her the other night on the cable outside our window. She was trying to get across to the grotesque. And the Committee was down in the street, watching her, like . . . like . . . they were cheering her on."

Pablo pictured Birdy, silent and still in the dark night air. He kept seeing Elmira Toledo's face on the television screen, and all the scientists standing like prison guards around the empty cage, and how they needed a real-life specimen. Maria tightened her arm around his shoulder, and he leaned into her. "Why don't you want her to fly, Pablo?"

"I do want her to fly! I mean, I don't want her to fly! I mean both!"

If Birdy would die without flying, then he wanted her to fly. But if it would leave him without her, without the one living being who had watched over him forever, then he didn't want her to fly.

Fortune lost and fortune gained. The winds of change. His mind was all jumbled up. He started crying, right there in the Critter Clinic. Birdy was no longer struggling against him, trying to get away. Now she was quiet in his arms, and Maria was still stroking her feathers, and Maria's arm was still around him.

"That's not the only thing," he said, swallowing a sob. He pushed his hand into his pocket and dragged out the feather. "There's this, too."

"Oh, Pablo. Did she give you this?"

Pablo nodded.

"She's in distress, then," Maria said. "She's trying to tell you something, Pablo. Something important."

Pablo closed his eyes. He was so, so tired all of a sudden. He knew what Birdy was trying to tell him, and what she was trying to tell him was that she needed to fly away. Or that she wanted to. But whether she wanted to or needed to, what was the difference?

If Birdy flew away, she would be gone.

TWENTY-NINE

IT WAS THE middle of the afternoon, but the OPEN sign on Pierre's was turned to CLOSED. The door was shut and the curtain drawn. Pablo knocked and kept on knocking until Pierre finally came to the door and pushed the curtain aside with a finger.

"It's Pablo," he called to the others, and then he unlocked the door. "We're strategizing," he said to Pablo. "Take a look."

Emmanuel was standing next to the PIERRE'S SPECIALS chalkboard, which was leaning up against the pastry case. Lula and Pierre were seated at the table. Emmanuel held a piece of blue chalk in his hands, and the chalkboard was filled with his spiky handwriting.

1. If Birdy is in fact a seafaring parrot, and if
2. Scientists and others are desperate to study a seafaring parrot, then
3. They will seize Birdy and keep her in an enclosed environment.
4. Seafaring parrots cannot survive in enclosed environments.

This was what it came down to. With a potential firsthand sighting like this one, surely already called in to the Tip Line by those bickering tourists who had zipped away after taking all those photos, Elmira Toledo would hightail it to Isla.

She would be the first on the scene—Elmira was always the first—but others would soon follow.

"Until we have a Seafarer in captivity . . ." said Elmira Toledo's voice.

They all jumped. The television was off and the screen dark. There was no way that Elmira Toledo had gotten there already, was there? They looked around the room and then at one another, bewildered.

"Until we have a Seafarer in captivity," said Elmira again.

But it wasn't Elmira. It was Birdy. She stood on the table, a frantic look in her dark eyes.

It was out of control at this point, Pablo could tell. She couldn't help herself anymore. She couldn't keep everything in, the way she must have been doing all these years. She closed her beak and ducked her head into her feathers, as if she hadn't meant to say anything. But more words emerged, and muffled though they were, with her head tucked under like that, everyone could still hear them. And everyone could also hear that they were Pablo's words, spoken in his voice.

"They'll lock her up in a cage. And Seafarers die if they're locked up in cages. Seafarers have to fly."

That's me, Pablo thought, *and I sound scared.* And it was true. He *was* scared.

The others were looking at him now, worry and sadness on their faces. Pablo picked up Birdy, pressed his nose into Birdy's feathers, and rocked her back and forth. Back and forth, back and forth, her dry, warm, dusty, mango-y smell filling his nose. Emmanuel put his hand on Pablo's knee.

"We all feel the same way, Pablito," he said.

Pierre clicked on the television. The real Elmira was on the screen, her purple glasses pushed back on her head.

"Viewers! This is Elmira Toledo, reporting live with breaking news on the elusive Seafaring Parrot! Not half an hour ago, two tourists called in from Isla to report a firsthand viewing, in a bakery, of a Seafarer in the flesh! I mean feathers! I mean a flesh bird with feathers in a bakery who was caught talking in a voice from the past!"

Elmira was so excited by the news that she couldn't keep her words straight. Beyond that, her trench coat was on inside out. Her hair was tousled and her eyes were wild. Someone off-screen must have signaled her at that point, because she took a deep breath and exhaled slowly.

"It is increasingly clear," she intoned, "that armed with this information, including the photos taken by our sharp-eyed tipsters, we may be on the verge of tracking down the first confirmed Seafaring Parrot in existence."

They all stared at the screen.

"What are we going to do?" said Pierre, looking to the others.

"We could put Toledo off the scent for a while," said Lula. "Or try, anyway."

"By hiding Birdy?"

"Maybe," said Emmanuel. "And by calling in

a bunch of fake tips from some other town."

"Stay tuned," Elmira was saying on the screen. "We will, of course, keep you apprised of any and all Seafarer developments."

Pierre clicked off the television. Birdy shifted in Pablo's arms, her gaze fixed on the closed door of Pierre's Goodies.

"What now?" said Pierre. "This is exactly as Darren Mandible said. Fortune lost."

"Don't be a doomsayer," said Lula. "That same fortune brought us our precocious baby, didn't it? Fortune gained."

Anger rose up inside Pablo, and he didn't try to stop it.

"I wasn't a precocious baby," he said. "That's just a stupid story. You all talk about my birthday, but no one even knows when my real birthday is. And none of you knows the truth of how I got here, or why."

Pablo's heart hammered inside his chest. These were things he had said only to Birdy, and only when they were down on the beach and no one could hear him. The others all looked at one another. Lula looked down at her mug of tea as if there were something she needed to figure out about it. Pierre folded his hands in his lap. No one said anything, and everyone looked sad. Emmanuel was the first to speak.

"Pablito," he said, "I didn't know you felt this way."

"Nor did I," said Pierre.

"Me either," said Lula.

"When you were little, I made up stories about how you ended up on the ocean because the thought of a little baby all alone out there was too . . . too . . ." Emmanuel hesitated.

"Sad," Lula said, finishing his sentence.

"We didn't want it to be a sad story," said Pierre.

"But it *is* sad," said Pablo. "It's happy because I'm here with all of you, but it's also sad."

He looked at all of them. Lula, Pierre, and Emmanuel here in the bakery with him. And Maria in the clinic. His family.

"Besides, I wasn't alone," he said. "Birdy was with me. I just wish I knew what happened. What *really* happened."

"Me too," Emmanuel said, "me too."

Birdy's dark eyes went from one to the other. She leaned forward from Pablo's arms, her wing raised as if she were ready to swat anyone who messed with him. But no one was messing with him. They were all listening. Now that he had started, Pablo couldn't stop.

"I'm not a pirate baby," he said. "I'm not a precocious baby. I'm not from a forgotten world. I don't know where I came from, and I don't know what happened to whoever I belonged to."

Emmanuel scooted his chair next to Pablo and put his arm around both him and Birdy.

"It was a time of upheaval when you came to us, Pablo," he said. His voice was slow and serious in a way that Pablo had never heard before, as if he were trying to find the exact right words. "Remember I told you about my family, and how they felt they couldn't stay where they were?"

Pablo nodded.

"What my parents went through is what many people went through," said Emmanuel. "What people are still going through, even right now, in other parts of the world. When you were a baby, there were stories everywhere of people trying to escape in boats from Cuba, little boats that weren't very safe, especially in a storm. And there was that huge storm, just a couple of days before you arrived. I figured you survived a wreck . . . that you were the only one to survive."

"You and Birdy," added Lula.

"It's a hard story," said Emmanuel. "I didn't want to hurt you. And I was so happy to have you, *mi Pablito*. I wanted it to be a happy story for my little boy."

"I'm not little anymore."

"But you used to be. Not even double digits, until now. That's what I've been trying to talk to you about. Maybe it's time to stop making up stories."

It's past time, Pablo thought. Then Birdy did

something. She dipped her head into the crook of Pablo's neck, plucked up the *Dios me bendiga* pendant with her beak, and pulled it out from under Pablo's T-shirt, so it was visible in the dim light of the bakery. She let the necklace drop back against Pablo's chest, and she began to speak, in Spanish, in the voice of that same woman.

Adios, mi dulce niño. Todo va a estar bien. Tu mamá te quiere. Todo va a estar bien.

Pablo didn't understand all the words—his Spanish wasn't very good—so he looked over at Emmanuel, whose Spanish was perfect. Birdy said the words again, in a soft voice, as soft as Emmanuel's when he translated them.

"Good-bye, my sweet boy. All will be well. Mama loves you. All will be well."

Birdy tilted her head, studying Emmanuel as if she wanted to make sure that he had translated the words right. Then she ducked her head into her feathers, the same way she had done his whole life whenever Pablo asked her about his story.

Adios mi
dulce niño
mamá
todo va
a estar bien

THIRTY

OUTSIDE IN THE alleyway, the dog startled awake. He was lying against the back door of the bakery, the place where he had stolen the elephant ears. Where he had heard the man's horrible voice, the voice that he thought he had gotten away from. Where the bird—the strange bird—had tried to make herself small, tried to keep her beak closed, tried to be silent.

But she was so full of noise. She couldn't hide it.

The little dog could hear it now, the sounds

inside the bird. They were coming at him right through the closed door.

Someone calling.

Someone screaming.

The roar of wind.

Crashing waves.

A baby's stuttering cry.

The groan and screech of wood pulling apart from nails and screws.

A woman's voice, low and hasty and full of sadness, saying human words that the dog could hear but didn't understand. *Adios, mi dulce niño. Todo va a estar bien. Tu mamá te quiere. Todo va a estar bien.*

The dog didn't want to hear any of this, but he couldn't help it. How horrible it must be to be that bird, that bird so full of noise and helpless to stop it.

THIRTY-ONE

THEY SAT TOGETHER for a while longer, all of them, in Pierre's bakery. Pablo held Birdy on his lap and then against his chest, as if she were a baby. He rocked her back and forth, the way he rocked himself to sleep in his hammock at night.

"I thought there would be more," he said at last. "There must be so much more."

Had he come from Cuba? Was his mother trying to leave there, with him, her baby? Had their boat foundered at sea in a storm? Had his mother been lost? Was Birdy with them both from the beginning, or had she found Pablo floating alone on the ocean and landed on the swimming pool to take care of him?

"Why did your family leave, Emmanuel?"

"Remember, Pablo? I told you they felt they couldn't stay anymore."

"Yes, but why, exactly?"

Emmanuel went quiet again, looking for the words. "They did not trust the new government," he said. "They were worried and afraid."

"My family too," said Lula. "Not Cuba, but Haiti. They were afraid."

"Mine too," Pierre said. "They weren't afraid of the government, but of starvation. This was a long time ago, in Ireland, during something called the potato famine, when many people died of hunger."

Cuba. Haiti. Ireland. Fear and distrust and starvation. *There is so much I don't know about,* Pablo thought. But at least Emmanuel and Lula and Pierre knew who their families were and where they had come from. Birdy had made herself small and silent, a ball of bird tucked up against his chest. Her head rested against his pendant.

"Birdy? Can you tell me more?" he whispered. "Can you tell me if it was my mother who gave me my necklace?"

She didn't move. Was she even listening? But then there was a faint push of a claw against his belly. She was listening, but she was silent. It must be so hard to hold all those sounds inside herself. Never to be able to unhear them. If she flew fast enough and high enough, could she outrace them? Was that why Seafarers never stopped flying?

"Pobrecita Birdy," he whispered. And then, to the others, "I'm going to Maria's."

THIRTY-TWO

"SHUT THE DOOR behind you, Pablo, will you?" Maria said. "And lock it, if you don't mind."

She must be as worried as everyone else about Birdy's safety. Elmira Toledo was exactly the kind of person that Maria kept her distance from. Maria didn't trust people who had "ulterior motives," as she called them. Pablo had never been exactly sure what that meant, but what he did know was that he trusted Maria, so he did as she said. She was sitting on the orange couch as if she had been waiting for them, the long blue-green feather that Birdy had plucked out and given to Pablo that morning in her hand. She handed it to him, and he slid it into his back pocket.

"What's going on?" said Maria.

He got straight to the point.

"If Birdy really is a Seafarer, then why can't she fly and why can't she talk?"

"She *can* talk. You've heard her."

"Not that kind of talk!" Pablo's voice was suddenly loud, even to his own ears. "Not other people's voices kind of talk! Not 'you worthless mutt' talk, or that voice that maybe is my mother and maybe isn't but who knows for sure and who ever will know for sure because, because . . ."

"Because what?"

"Because Birdy won't tell me!"

Pablo felt mean. And something else. He felt angry. As if she sensed his anger, Birdy jumped off his shoulder and landed with a small *thud* on the other side of Maria. "And that makes me mad!" he said. "All this time—all these years—

she's known my story? And she never told me?"

Pablo turned to Birdy. "All those times I told you how much I wanted to know my story, and you knew? You *knew*?"

He had never been angry at Birdy before, and it was a terrible feeling. Terrible to see her gaze back at him with that look of . . . of . . . "Don't look so sad, Birdy!" He was yelling now, but he could not stop. So many years of wondering, and she had known all along? "If you can talk, you should have told me! You *knew*!"

His hands were shaking, and Maria took them and held them between her own.

"Pablo," she said, "have you considered that it may not be her fault?"

"How could it *not* be her fault?" Oh, he sounded spiteful, but he couldn't help it. His bird! She had known all this time—his whole life!—and she hadn't told him!

"Maybe she wanted to tell you, but she couldn't," said Maria.

"What are you *saying*? And if she couldn't tell

me, then you should know why, shouldn't you? You're the doctor."

Listen to me, Pablo thought, *so rude,* and then the equally awful thought came to him that Birdy would hear him talking like this forever, inside her head. Forever! Pablo instantly sat up straight and quiet. Maria was still holding his hands.

"What I'm saying," said Maria, "is that maybe Birdy knows your story, but for some unknown reason, she can't tell it to you."

At that, Birdy tilted her head and looked straight at Pablo, as if she agreed with Maria.

"Let's look at what we both know for sure," said Maria. Her voice was calm and matter-of-fact. That must be the scientist in her, coming out in a time of stress. "We know that in the ten years she's been here, Birdy has not flown. She's never even made an attempt to fly, correct?"

"Not until the other night, when I found her out on the cable. She hasn't talked, either." Thinking about how she hadn't talked, not in all these years, even when she *could* talk, made the anger come rising back up in Pablo, but he took a deep breath and focused. "Except for now, I mean, and a little bit in her sleep."

"Did she always talk in her sleep? Ever since you can remember?"

Pablo shook his head. "No. It's only been the last couple of weeks."

"Okay. Why, then, would she suddenly start to talk in her sleep? And why all this talk, a flood of it, today? There must be some reason. Something must have changed."

Birdy was quiet and still, as if she were interested in the conversation and wanted to see where it might lead.

"I have no idea," said Pablo. "The only thing that's different is that I'm about to turn double digits. And why would that matter?"

But even as he was talking, the image of Darren Mandible flashed into his head, dipping and swirling in front of his weather map, so excited was he at the thought of the winds of change. And Elmira Toledo, her trench coat blowing open in the gale. The scientists. The Tip Line. He turned to Maria just as she turned to him.

"The winds—" he said.

"Of change!" she finished. "Listen, Pablo. There's a principle in science known as Occam's razor, which holds that the simplest explanation is usually the right one."

"So could that mean that the winds of change are why Birdy's talking? And trying to fly?"

"Well, according to Occam's razor, that would make sense."

Birdy pushed her beak into Maria's shoulder and then hopped over and did the same to Pablo's shoulder, as if to encourage them. Pablo stroked her feathers. His anger was gone. He was thinking, thinking hard.

"Maybe the only time Birdy can talk and fly is when the winds of change are here?" he said. "Sort of talk, anyway? And try to fly?"

"I'm wondering the same thing," said Maria.

They sat there, the three of them, Maria and

Pablo and Birdy. It was quiet on the street outside, which was unusual. No alpacas or ferrets or stray cats or teddy bears in the office today, which was also unusual. Did the winds of change make everything weird and strange and not like usual? Birdy pushed her beak into his shoulder again, but sharply this time. Then she nipped at his ear.

"Ouch," said Pablo. "That hurts."

But she did it again.

"Birdy, if you want something, why don't you just tell me what it is?" he said. "Can't you do that?"

Jab. Again with her sharp beak, this time right on his chin, which was not like her at all. She must be trying to tell him something, but why she didn't just *tell* him was . . . wait a minute. Pablo's mind whisked through the events of the last week. Birdy had inched out on the cable, but she hadn't actually flown. She had poured forth sounds and voices, jumbled and chaotic, but she hadn't actually said anything that came directly from *her*, had she? She had not said, for example,

Pablo, I am going to tell you the story of what really happened to you, and to me, and why we ended up on that tiny inflatable swimming pool, had she?

No. She had not.

Just the thought of Birdy saying something like that brought tears to Pablo's eyes. If only she would. He looked at her, at her steady dark eyes fixed on his, at the tilt of her head. At her lavender feathers with iridescent blue-green under-feathers, so beautiful and so unearthly. Surely, if there were any way for Birdy to speak to him in her own voice, to tell him the true story of his beginnings, she would do so. She had taken care of him his whole life, after all. Pablo turned to Maria.

"Maybe she can only make sounds that she's already heard?" he said, trying to puzzle it out. "Maybe only when the winds of change are here? That would be the simplest explanation, wouldn't it?"

"It would," said Maria. "You'd make a good scientist, Pablo."

Pablo remembered the awful sound of the man's voice in his room in the middle of the night. He remembered the frightened look in Birdy's eyes in the bakery, when she hadn't been able to stop bringing forth voices. He remembered the night he had found her inching out on the cable, high above the street. If his theory was right, and Birdy could speak only during the winds of change, then maybe she could fly only during the winds of change as well.

As if she could read his mind, Birdy hopped onto his lap. She pushed her beak into his neck, but gently this time. "Maybe only when the winds of change are here?" she said, in his own voice, the same question he had asked just minutes before. That must be the closest she could come to telling them that they were right. That he and Maria had figured it out.

Pablo thought of all the mornings he had almost-flown her down the beach, and how much she loved it. He thought of the legend of the Seafaring Parrot, the great heights it climbed to and the vast distances it covered at sea. Then he pictured Elmira Toledo and her crew descending on Isla, determined to find a living specimen.

"I need some time to figure out what to do," he said to Maria, and she nodded.

THIRTY-THREE

OUTSIDE, THE WIND was picking up. There was something strange about it, and when Pablo realized what the strangeness was, his heart beat harder in his chest. Darren Mandible had been right. The wind was beginning to blow directly away from the shore.

"What day is it?" came a quiet voice.

Pablo looked down. The Committee was gathered on the sidewalk outside the Critter Clinic. Mr. Chuckles advanced a step toward Pablo, as if he had been chosen to lead this meeting.

"Shoo," said Pablo. "Leave us alone. I'm trying to figure something out here."

The Committee didn't move. Dumb birds, scratching and clucking around the town, free to go where they wanted to whenever they wanted to. Unlike Birdy, who had never left Pablo's side but for that one time, out on the cable. Who did the Committee think they were? They were nothing special. Nothing like Birdy.

"You guys think you can talk," said Pablo. He knew he sounded mean, but he didn't stop himself. "But all you do is say the same things over and over again. That doesn't make you special."

"HAHAHAHAHA!" said Mr. Chuckles.

"You laugh, but why?" said Pablo. "There's nothing funny about this situation! How would *you* like to be locked up in a cage for the rest of your life?"

The birds looked at one another and then back at Pablo. Mr. Chuckles cocked his head.

"Hmm," he said. "Hmm. Hmm. Hmm."

It was as if he was trying to tell Pablo something. But what?

"'Hmm' is not going to get you very far, now is it?" said Pablo. He just kept saying mean things.

The other birds cocked their heads, blinked, opened and closed their beaks. All except Rhody, who just kept scratching the same little place on the sidewalk, as if he were tapping out some kind of avian Morse code.

Pablo didn't know what to do.

He thought back over all the years he and Birdy had been together, and all the times he had told her the things he couldn't tell Emmanuel or anyone else. Things about his non-birthday. About his *Dios me bendiga* necklace. About his own ideas of where he might have come from, and why he had been set upon the ocean alone. Birdy knew all his secrets.

She was quiet against his chest.

Something about her silence and her stillness unnerved him. Her eyes were fixed on something in the sky. He followed her gaze upward. The cable swayed high above them, a gray snake, and across the chasm of the air, small birds swooped back and forth. The babies, those who had survived the weeks of learning to fly, were all bigger now. Still smaller than their parents, but big enough to pop out of the nests on their own, diving and darting for food. Pablo looked at Birdy; her eyes were steady. She wasn't following the fly lines of the little birds.

Was she looking at the grotesque?

Maybe. It was impossible to tell. Together they stood, looking up. The steel cable began to shimmer, undulating back and forth. Pablo heard the building around him groan and sigh. Then, and Pablo would swear this for the rest of his life, the grotesque shifted on the stone ledge. It turned, was what happened, it turned its head high in the air above them, and as Pablo watched in disbelief, muscles rippled under its scaly stone chest. Its wings lifted ever so slightly from its sides, and—Pablo swore this—it hunched forward, until it looked to Pablo as if the grotesque was about to fling itself off the ledge it had been cemented onto for as long as he could remember. The same way Birdy had hunched forward on the table at Maria's not long ago.

Birdy struggled up to Pablo's shoulder and dug her talons in. Her own wings lifted ever so slightly from her sides. Emmanuel's words came back to Pablo, that the grotesque was there to watch over the animals and birds of Isla. About how it was neither living nor dead, stuck forever there on its stone ledge.

THIRTY-FOUR

THE STREETS OF Isla were curiously quiet, almost as quiet as they got when a wild storm was headed their way. No one was boarding up their windows or sandbagging their storefront doors, but still, the uneasy feeling inside Pablo seemed to be in the very air of the town itself. Pablo tucked Birdy underneath his T-shirt to hide her, something she ordinarily would never have put up with, but she rested against his chest and didn't move. He left the Committee behind, scratching and clucking, then crossed the street and went down the block to Pierre's Goodies, where the blinds were still drawn. Pablo had to knock three times before Lula peeked out and unlocked the door for him.

"Quick," she said, and she drew the bolt again once he was inside. Birdy poked her head out of the top of Pablo's T-shirt in greeting, but made no move otherwise.

Elmira Toledo was holding forth on the television screen. Her hair was brushed today, and her trench coat was buttoned all the way to her neck, but if you looked closely, there was still a manic gleam in her eye. She appeared to be standing on a promontory of some sort, huge waves crashing ominously behind her.

"Rest assured, viewers, that the Tip Line Hounds have been following up on each and every credible report of a Seafarer sighting," she said.

"Tip Line Hounds?" Lula said. "That's a new one."

"A new and nasty one," Pierre said. "An

insult to the good name of dogs worldwide."

Pierre had never been one to either notice or compliment any of the Isla dogs, and he protected his pastries against strays with an iron fist. Just look at how he'd gone running after the little elephant-ear thief, and how grudgingly he'd put out food for him only when Lula pressured him into it. It seemed that the winds of change were changing everything.

"An extremely credible tip came in just last night," Elmira was saying, "and that is why my camera crew and I find ourselves here on the Outer Banks."

"Mon dieu!" said Pierre. "That was my tip! I called that one in!"

His face turned red with pride. Just then a particularly enormous wave crested the promontory and drenched Elmira, who managed to hang grimly on to her microphone nonetheless.

"Sadly, our search here has proved fruitless," she said. "But we are hot on the trail of another highly credible tip, one which will take us to the top of a lighthouse on St. Sabrina's Island off the Florida Panhandle."

"That's my tip!" said Lula. "I called it in anonymously from the pay phone outside the Parrot Café. I said I was the lighthouse keeper on St. Sabrina's, and there was a Seafarer swooping around and around the lighthouse in such a wild manner that I was afraid it was deranged and in need of hospitalization. Good one, right?"

It certainly was. Everyone looked at Lula admiringly. For better, and once in a while for worse, she never held back. Meanwhile, on the screen, Elmira was clutching the microphone with both hands. Her teeth were chattering. The Outer Banks, or at least her particular promontory thereof, did not look hospitable in the least.

"We leave momentarily and will be back with a live report early this afternoon," she said, shivering. "Stay tuned, viewers, for further developments."

Emmanuel clicked off the television. "Well, we've bought ourselves some time," he said. "But how much?"

"Not enough," said Lula darkly.

No one disagreed.

That evening, as the sky outside their window turned purple and then black with nightfall, the winds of change descended fully on Isla. A ghostly moon appeared and disappeared behind swift clouds, so that the ocean sparkled and then went black, sparkled and went black. The steel cable stretching between their building and the grotesque's stone ledge glimmered. Pablo's hammock rocked back and forth, and he picked up Birdy and crawled into it and pulled his blanket tight around them both.

Not so he could try to sleep, though. No, he needed to think. But his thoughts were still all jumbled up. The only thing that was steady was the wind. He could feel the whole building leaning, leaning toward the ocean.

Birdy's talons gripped his hands lightly. Together they swayed back and forth in the hammock. He put his arms around her, there in the rocking hammock, there in the dark night, there in the building that groaned and swayed from the winds of change, and he breathed in a long, deep breath. Warmth and dust and the faint smell of mangoes. The smell of Birdy.

The feather she had pulled from herself that morning was still in the back pocket of Pablo's shorts. He thought of the years she had stayed beside him, never leaving his side. He thought of Elmira Toledo, and the scientists with their clipboards, and the tourists desperate for the sight of a Seafaring Parrot. Then he thought of the night he had found her halfway across the street, balanced on the cable. He thought and thought, and as he thought, his mind became clear.

It was time.

He held her to his chest and swung his legs out of the hammock. The clouds were gone now, and stars glittered high in the heavens, impervious to the wind that was bending the palm trees toward the ocean as far as Pablo could see. It was the sort of stormless wind that the townspeople had talked about as long as Pablo could remember. The winds that blew not onto shore but away from it were the winds that would carry his bird away.

Somewhere out there, airplanes were winging their way through the night. Maybe Elmira Toledo had realized that Lula's lighthouse tip was a hoax and was on one of those airplanes, bound for Isla and a real live specimen. He squinted and peered into the darkness, trying to see if he could make out any light on the ocean that wasn't from the stars or moon. No. It was just him and . . . wait.

Wait.

What was that in the sky, far out to sea, making its way south toward them? It couldn't be a plane, because it was flying too low. Whatever it was, it was growing closer every second. Then Pablo's ears picked up a sound that wasn't the wind. It sounded a little like Emmanuel's snores when he really got going, but it wasn't quite that, either. He concentrated on the approaching object and the growing sound—

Helicopter. That's what it was.

Emmanuel had been right in that they had bought themselves time, but Lula had been righter. There was only one person who would be crazy enough—or greedy enough was a better term—to board a helicopter bound for Isla in the crosswinds of the winds of change. Elmira Toledo was here. Pablo's heart began to hammer in his chest. This was too soon. He needed more time with Birdy. He needed at least a few hours. He needed . . . he needed . . . he tried not to think about the future, but he couldn't help it.

Who would stand on the counter pecking at diced mango while he made quesadillas? Who would look on when he played rummy with Emmanuel, hopping back and forth to study their cards and pointing with her beak at the one she wanted Pablo to discard? Who would listen to his secrets down at the beach, at the very edge of the ocean?

Birdy pushed her beak into the crook of his neck as if she knew what he was thinking. He stroked her feathers from the top of her head to the tip of her tail and kept his eyes on the approaching helicopter. It was hovering on the outskirts of town now, battling against the off-shore gale. In the bright light of the moon he could make out large neon script that spelled TOLEDO TIP LINE. Any minute now, the helicopter would be on the ground, and Elmira would begin a relentless search for the fabled Seafarer. Birdy was in imminent danger.

Pablo took a deep breath, and through his panicked sadness, he forced his voice to be calm and strong.

"Listen," he said. "If you get lonely out there"—he waved his hand at the sky, the enormous sky beyond the window—"listen to our voices, okay?"

Her talons tightened on his skin. She was listening.

"Listen to Emmanuel telling the pirate baby story, and Lula talking about how no one should get a tattoo that lasts forever, and Maria with the

alpacas, and Pierre yelling at the pastry thief—" Here he stopped, because she suddenly dug her claws in so tight that they hurt.

"Hey," he said. "That hurts."

But she dug in harder.

"Are you trying to tell me something again?" he said. "What about? Lula? Emmanuel? Pierre and the pastry—" *Ouch!* There she went again. She was telling him something about the pastry thief.

"The dog?"

Ouch. Yes. That was it.

And then she spoke. *"Pobrecito perrito."* The voice she spoke in was familiar, because it was Pablo's own voice, from a few days ago. Birdy's head was tilted and her dark eyes watchful, as if she wanted him to understand something about the little dog.

"Whatever it is you want me to do, I'll figure it out," he said. "I promise."

They looked out the window. The fronds of the palm trees streamed seaward in the wind. The helicopter was lowering itself, a giant ungainly insect, onto the beach two blocks away. The door popped open and Elmira Toledo, bent low to avoid the blades, her trench coat blowing open in the wild wind, ran across the sand. She was followed closely by her camera crew.

"You ready, Birdy?" he said. He had to keep his voice steady for her sake. He didn't want her flying away with the sound of him crying in her ears, to stay with her forever. She gripped his arm again with her talons. She was ready.

"Think how great it will be when you're back in the sky," he said. His voice did not tremble. He did not cry. He was doing this for her. "The winds of change will hold you up, and you'll spread your wings, and you'll fly back out over the ocean. And if you miss me, or Emmanuel, or Lula or Pierre, or Maria, you know what to do."

Pablo held Birdy with one hand and reached around to the back of his neck with the other. It took a while to unknot the leather cord. It had never been off his neck before. He folded his fingers around the pendant for the last time, then kissed it.

"Hold tight," he said to Birdy, and she did. *"Dios te bendiga."*

Then he wrapped the cord around his bird's neck and laced it underneath her feathers so it wouldn't impede her flight. Her talons dug into his arm and he opened the window. He was so used to the breeze blowing in through the screen that the absence of it was startling. The silk-screened fake parrot on the banner flapped wildly from the cable. The palm trees were still bent nearly in half, leaning toward the sea, and no birds darted back and forth across the chasm of the street.

"Here we go," he said.

He placed her on the windowsill. She lurched forward, immediately caught off guard by the force of the wind. Pablo's arms shot out and he grabbed her up just in time. His heart hammered in his chest. This wasn't going to work. She didn't have enough room to spread her wings and catch

the wind, not when she hadn't flown in so long. Maybe she wouldn't remember how, and she would just fall straight to the street below.

He thought of the baby birds who hadn't made it. He couldn't let that happen to his Birdy. Across the way, the grotesque stared at them, its stone body rigid.

The grotesque's stone ledge, unlike their narrow windowsill, had enough room for a bird to catch the current. Pablo unhooked the hammock from the wall. Before he could think too much about what he was about to do, he was crawling out through the open window and hooking the hammock to the steel cable. It twitched under his hands, sending that electric feeling prickling through his body.

"All will be well," he said to Birdy, and then he said it again to himself, kind of like a prayer. *All will be well. All will be well.*

With Birdy tucked under his arm, Pablo eased himself into the hammock—*be brave,* he told himself, *don't think about it*—and folded the mesh up tight around the two of them. He looked down, but only for a second. It was far too far to the street below. He looked up instead. The moon shone steady despite the rushing wind, and that gave him strength. *All will be well,* he told himself, *all will be well.* Birdy settled into his arms, there in the hammock in the sky.

Pablo reached up and gave a tentative tug on the cable. He and Birdy dangled above the dark street, but the hooks held, and the cable held, and across the dark chasm they went. Inch by inch, gradually gaining ground and speed as Pablo saw that his plan was working. *All will be well, all will be well*—with each chant he hauled them farther across the street, until they reached the banner. He took his pocketknife from his back pocket and sawed at the banner until a slit opened up. The wind took it from there, ripping the banner from its moorings in a matter of seconds. Pablo watched it twist and writhe in the wind, a phantom bird descending to the street below. He hauled the hammock onward.

There was a sudden commotion far, far below on the street. Pablo glanced down and beheld the Committee swarming around Elmira Toledo. She had already made it to their street! Peaches was nipping at her ankles. Sugar Baby kept fluttering up and down, as if she were a tiny avian basketball guard and Elmira the opposing center. Mr. Chuckles kept laughing—HAHAHAHAHA—but there was a dangerous sound to his laughter, and no matter how frantically Elmira Toledo windmilled her arms to shoo the Committee away, they stayed put.

"Quickly now, Birdy," Pablo whispered in her ear.

There was no time to waste. One tug after another, as smoothly as he could, Pablo hauled the hammock onward as the Committee kept Elmira at bay.

Then they were at the stone ledge. The mud nests of the birds were dark shadows underneath the overhang. Directly above the giant hook that held the steel cable tight across the street, the grotesque's talons protruded.

"We made it, Birdy. We're here."

She knew what to do. She was already crawling out of the hammock, talons hooking themselves into the mesh while she balanced with her wings. She couldn't make it over the overhang, though, and Pablo reached his arm out.

"Step up," he said, but the wind whipped his words away. Birdy stepped up anyway, and then, as she balanced there between the grotesque's ledge and the swaying hammock, she looked down at him. The pendant gleamed, half-hidden in the downy feathers of her chest.

Be brave, he told himself one last time.

"Good-bye, Birdy-bird," he said. "All will be well. Pablo loves you."

She swayed on the grotesque's clawed foot, balanced on the very edge of the ledge, and lifted her wings slightly from her sides. She leaned forward, and he knew she was trying to catch the wind just right, so that it would lift beneath her and sail her out across the buildings, past the bent-double palm trees, out over the ocean.

Beyond the far edge of the town, the sea shone in fractured bits of light. Birdy leaned farther, and farther again, and then she spread her wings wide and let the wind take her.

She winged her way out over the ocean she had floated in on so long ago, and then she was gone.

DIOS
ME
BENDIGA

THIRTY-FIVE

THE LITTLE DOG had fallen back asleep in the alleyway. His head rested on a piece of broken cement. He had spent some time that night trying to tear the burrs and thorns from his fur with his teeth and paws, but his coat was too long and matted and he gave up.

As he slept, the little dog nosed and scrabbled and sighed and panted. Maybe something was chasing him in his dream. Maybe he was trying to hide from someone. Maybe he was hungry, too hungry to sleep well. He had escaped from the awful house, but now he had no home at all.

The strange wind that was blowing with so much force everywhere else in the town did not reach him, there in the narrow alley.

He woke from his restless dreams just in time to see a strange sight. High above him, in the bit of dark sky visible between the tall walls, a bird was soaring in an upward spiral. Up and up and up she flew, a bright small something glimmering in her feathers.

THIRTY-SIX

THAT FIRST MORNING, the first day without Birdy, Pablo walked out the door of his apartment building alone. He had slept very late, and Emmanuel had left a note on the kitchen table.

I'll be at Pierre's with the others, mi Pablito. Come down when you wake up.

Pablo's shoulder felt empty without Birdy balancing on it. He was so used to her warm weight and the grip of her talons. The minute he stepped outside he wasn't alone, though. The Committee squawked and gabbled at the sight of him, as if they had been waiting. They all talked at once, fluttering around his ankles.

"Cock-a-doodle-doo! Cock-a-doodle-doo!"

Rhody seemed intent on something, going so far as to peck at Pablo's toes.

"Hey," he said. "Stop that."

"Watch what you're saying!" squawked Peaches. "Simmer down, simmer down!"

Sugar Baby even flew a little spiral around his head, seeming to surprise herself by doing so, and unfortunately landed on Peaches's head.

"What day is it?" she said. "What day is it?"

"A hard one, Sugar," Pablo said.

She cocked her head and looked up at him with her bright eyes. They all did. The Committee drove him crazy sometimes, but right now Pablo felt grateful for their presence. They had been down there on the street last night, after all. They had all watched what happened, all watched as Birdy flew away.

But there seemed to be something else on their minds. They kept fluttering around and then hopping a few feet down the sidewalk, as if there was something they wanted to show him. Peaches took the lead, half marching and half fluttering. The others followed in her wake, not even stopping to linger outside Pierre's, even though the door was open and Pierre was visible behind the counter.

"Simmer down, simmer down!" Peaches called back, craning her neck to make sure that Pablo was following. Which he was.

She halted at the entrance to the alleyway, and the others did too. They fluttered forward an inch or two, then back an inch or two, gradually moving forward until the entire Committee was clustered at the dark entrance.

"What is it?" said Pablo. "What's going on?"

They all started talking at once.

"Watch what you're saying!"

"HAHAHAHAHA!"

"Cock-a-doodle-doo!"

And, underneath the others, the quiet murmur of "What day is it? What day is it?"

Pablo made his way through the feathers and clucks to the entrance of the alleyway. And there he saw the little dog, his head resting on a chunk of broken cement. His fur was so matted and dirty and long that it was hard to tell which end was up. But he was sound asleep, and this was Pablo's chance. He had made a promise to Birdy, after all. So he took one big step forward and—lightning quick, before the dog could wake up and zoom away—scooped him up in both arms. With the Committee on his heels, he hauled the struggling dog across the street to Maria's.

"Maria?" he called through the door, and arms clamped around the wiggly, terrified dog, waited as she opened it and let them in. All of them.

"Pablo?" she said. There was a question in her eyes, but he avoided looking at her. He couldn't talk about Birdy yet.

"The dog," he said.

"Oh yes," said Maria. "The dog. Poor little guy."

The dog calmed down the minute Maria's

hands were on him. She had that effect on animals. Pablo and the Committee watched as she felt through his fur, both hands gentle but firm, looking for wounds or broken bones. Then she flipped up his long ears and peered into them with her otoscope. She pried open his mouth and checked his teeth. Finally she examined his lopsided tail.

"He's a mess," she said, "but messes can be cleaned up."

"How did he break his tail? Can you tell?"

"I have no idea, other than that it happened a long time ago. Beyond that, it's a mystery."

She looked at him and smiled. "Which gives you something in common with each other, doesn't it?"

When Pablo didn't say anything, Maria reached out and touched his shoulder, the same shoulder that Birdy always rode on, and he knew that she knew.

"You know what would make Birdy happy, Pablo?"

Pablo and Maria looked at each other, and then at the Committee, who were quiet for once, watching and waiting. They all looked at the little dog. He looked back at them. And then, Maria's arms still holding him steady, his lopsided tail began to wag back and forth.

"HAHAHAHAHA!"

"Cock-a-doodle-doo!"

"What day is it?"

"A good day to give a little dog a home," said Maria, "that's what day it is."

She placed the dog in Pablo's arms. He bent his head to the dog's fur and breathed in. He didn't smell good. At all. But he did smell warm. And dusty. And a tiny bit like . . . elephant ears.

THIRTY-SEVEN

IN THE WEEKS to come, the little dog would learn many things.

He would learn that while dog food and elephant ears and fried plantains and bits of roast meat were good, baked sweet potatoes were even better. And that carrots might be the best of all . . . next to cheese quesadillas, that is, even though Pablo would only give him little pieces of quesadilla because, according to Maria, they weren't very good for dogs. He would learn that a big soft cushion on the floor next to Pablo's hammock made a wonderful bed. He would learn that he was a good dancer when Emmanuel would pick him up and swing him around the kitchen to the sounds of the Buena Vista Social Club. He would learn that he was a good worker when, in the debris-strewn week that followed the departure of the winds of change, he would help the citizens of Isla clean up by inspecting all manner of spilled trash, especially spilled food scraps.

He would learn that the world was not only loud voices saying mean things, it was also soft voices saying kind things. To him. Yes, even to him.

Things like, "Are you thirsty, little guy?"

And "Do you need your belly scratched?"

And "Want to go for a walk?"

To all these things the little dog would learn to say YES, which in his case took the form of turning in a fast circle, chasing his lopsided tail until he fell right down on the floor. But even that wouldn't be so bad, for whoever was on the other end of the question would pick him right up and make sure he was okay.

He would also learn that he had a name. It wasn't the name he had been born with, if he had ever had one besides WORTHLESS MUTT, that is. His name would be given to him a few days after Emmanuel and Pablo adopted him, when they were giving him a haircut.

At first, Emmanuel would try to trim out the burrs and matted tufts, but there were too many of them. So he would end up cutting off the little dog's fur, until he was a shivery skinny thing standing on the kitchen floor, tangled piles of fur rising around him.

"Osito," Emmanuel would say. "That's what all that fur made you look like, a little bear."

Within a day everyone on the block would know him as Osito. It was a good name.

When Pablo and Maria walked into Pierre's the morning after Birdy flew away, in the company of the scruffy little dog but not Birdy, Emmanuel was the first to figure out what Pablo had done.

"Pablo," he said. *"Mi Pablito."*

He stood up and folded Pablo into his arms. The others sat at the table, the chalkboard filled up again with possibilities for hiding Birdy, for keeping her permanently hidden from the likes of Elmira Toledo.

"Where's Birdy?" said Pierre, not understanding.

Lula stayed silent, looking from Pablo to the back door of the bakery, as if there were a clue there. Maria, wise Maria, looked at Pablo and smiled a sad smile. Then she went to the front door and pushed back the curtain and looked out, up at the sky, as if hoping to see something. But the sky was clear. Pablo put his hand to his T-shirt and felt for the new pendant he was wearing, the pendant he had stayed up the rest of the night to make. It was a new Painted Parrot seashell that he had made with special waterproof paint and strung on a leather cord, a tiny painting of a beautiful bird winging her way across a dark sky, a bird with lavender feathers and dark eyes, a bird trailing a nearly invisible blessing necklace behind her. This seashell painting had no need of a caption.

Lula squinted in surprise. "That's a brand-new necklace you're wearing, isn't it?" she said, and Pablo nodded. She leaned over to examine it, turning the little seashell this way and that so it caught the light. Then she kissed her finger and wordlessly touched it to the tiny painted bird.

In the days after Birdy's departure, they comforted themselves by laughing at the funny news footage Elmira Toledo's camera crew had taken of her battling back the fierce Committee, and how satisfying her disappointment at finding no live specimen of the legendary parrot had been. How Darren Mandible was much shorter in person than on television, and how disappointed *he* was that the winds of change had lasted less than a day. They tried not to laugh out loud when Mr. Chuckles looked Elmira in her trench coat and Darren in his disco pants up and down, as if they were churchgoers on Sunday morning, and let loose with a "HAHAHAHAHA!" They looked forward to the return of the marine expedition, which had been blown off course by the winds of change, and to filling Oswaldo and the others in on how funny it had been. They liked watching the end of the Special Seafaring Report, which featured the same scientists grouped around the same empty cage and frowning.

"May it stay empty forever," said Maria, and everyone applauded.

THIRTY-EIGHT

"EMMANUEL," SAID PABLO a few days after Birdy's departure, "I want to talk to you about something."

Emmanuel had made arroz con pollo for dinner, and now he and Pablo stood at the sink washing dishes with the Buena Vista Social Club playing softly in the background. Plate by plate, bowl by bowl, pan by pan, Emmanuel washed and Pablo dried. Nothing was different and everything was different, with no Birdy standing on the counter next to them.

"I'm listening, Pablito," Emmanuel said, and he took the dish towel from Pablo's hand and dried the last pan. Pablo took a deep breath. If Birdy were here, she would flutter up to his shoulder and the feel of her talons holding on tight would be a comfort. But she wasn't here. *Be brave,* he told himself.

"I'm sad that I won't ever see my first family," said Pablo. "Or hear their stories, or know what they look like or sound like, except for, for . . . the sound of my mother's voice when she let me go. And I hope that doesn't hurt your feelings."

"Why would it hurt my feelings?"

"Because you're my family, Emmanuel. You and Birdy and Lula and Pierre and Maria, all of you."

"We *are* your family, *mi Pablito,*" said Emmanuel. "But that doesn't mean you're not sad about what you lost. I feel sad because I wish I could help you, but I don't have answers either."

Emmanuel leaned down and put his hands on Pablo's shoulders. Pablo took a deep breath and let it out slowly. The weight of his fingers wasn't like Birdy's talons, but it wasn't that far off, either.

"But one thing to remember, Pablito, is that others share your story."

"They do?" Pablo tried not to sound skeptical, but it was hard to imagine that there were other people out there who had floated in to shore on an inflatable pool, with a bird watching over them. Emmanuel smiled, as if he knew what Pablo was thinking.

"Not exactly like your story," he said. "But remember that there are many others in this world who had to leave their homes, for various reasons, and their journeys are long and hard."

Then, as big as Pablo was—almost double digits—Emmanuel picked him up as if he were little again and hugged him tight. "What do you say to a game of rummy?" he said.

Pablo wasn't sure how he felt about a game of rummy, to be honest. It wouldn't be the same without Birdy hopping from one side of the table to the other, inspecting their cards and advising them with a point of her beak or a swat of her wing. But he nodded anyway. Emmanuel shuffled and Pablo dealt, and the Buena Vista Social Club played on in the background.

It was the day after they all celebrated Pablo's maybe-birthday—that was what they decided to call it—with chocolate cake and strawberry ice cream, that Pablo caught a glimpse of a new tattoo on Lula's arm, peeking out from under her sleeve.

"What's that?" he said. "The special of the day?"

"Kind of."

"Can I see?"

She rolled her sleeve up and didn't say anything. Pablo did, though.

"Birdy," he said. Because there she was, an exact replica of his new painted seashell necklace. His bird, her wings spread, soaring through the air, the pendant blessing flying behind her.

"How did you know I gave it to her?" he said, pointing at the necklace in the tattoo.

"Because the morning after she flew away, you walked into the bakery with that new necklace," said Lula. "And I knew."

Pablo studied the tattoo. It was beautiful, simple black lines on Lula's brown arm.

"I told you I was going to make you a special tattoo for your birthday," she said. "Remember?"

Pablo nodded. Then he looked closer.

"Wait a minute," he said. "This doesn't look like henna."

"It's not."

"I thought you didn't believe in permanent tattoos."

She shrugged. "I was wrong. Some tattoos are worth keeping forever."

She rolled her sleeve back down and winked at him.

"One, anyway."

Weeks and months later, Pablo sometimes woke in the night and automatically looked over at the old Cuba suitcase to check on Birdy. But there was never a bird perched on top of it, and then he would remember that she was gone. She would not be back.

Pablo would lie in his hammock and pull his blanket tight around him. He would reach out to the wall and set the hammock rocking, just a little bit, back and forth, the way he had been doing all his life.

Sometimes Osito, on the big cushion on the floor next to his hammock, would sigh in his sleep. Osito was a busy sleeper, one who often sighed or yelped or moved his legs as if he were running in his sleep. Pablo liked to think that he was dreaming of elephant ears, racing down the sidewalk to escape Pierre and his wrath. Maybe not, though. Maybe he was remembering a time before he came to live here in this town, with Emmanuel and Pablo. Pablo would never know.

He would reach down and stroke Osito's

belly as he slept. Now that his fur was grown in, it was soft and silky. His ribs were no longer sharp sticks, about to poke through his sides. He stretched and sighed in his sleep as Pablo stroked his belly from chest to leg, over and over.

Pablo also felt for his collar, half-hidden beneath the silky fur. He had made it for Osito himself, from the feather that Birdy had given him and a leather cord. Emmanuel had made a tag for it in the shape of an elephant ear. If you looked at it in a certain way, an elephant ear looked remarkably like a heart, Pablo thought. And that seemed right.

Sometimes he lay awake for a long time, stroking Osito's fur as he slept on, until the sky began to grow light and Rhody, far below, crowed. The grotesque across the way was in its usual position, talons gripping the edge of the ledge, its eyes shadowed and deep. Soon the baby birds would begin their perilous tumbles from the mud nests, their parents swooping back and forth nervously. Soon the block below would fill with people needing their coffee and pastry from Pierre's Goodies, their henna tattoos from Lula Tattoo, their maps and T-shirts and Pablo's Painted Parrot seashells from Seafaring Souvenirs.

Yes, the block below would soon be bustling and noisy.

But not yet.

It was during that quiet time, neither night nor morning, that Pablo would imagine where his bird might be.

Was she flying right now? Was she out there, far away, somewhere on the vast stretch of the ocean? Was she high up, almost to the clouds, as high as legend said Seafarers could fly? Was she lonely? Did she ever bring back his voice, to keep her company as she flew? Did she sometimes listen in on him now, when he talked with Emmanuel or Lula or Pierre or Oswaldo, or when the Committee got out of line and he had to reprimand them?

"Birdy-bird," he would whisper, there in the

stillness of his room, in the back-and-forth hammock. "Birdy-bird."

Then he would tip himself out of his hammock, and Osito would stretch and yawn on his big cushion, and together the two of them would head to the kitchen to make strong coffee and bring a mug of it to Emmanuel.

What Pablo had not expected was that Birdy's voice would come back to him too. When he missed her the most—making quesadillas, or watching Emmanuel dance Osito around the room to the Buena Vista Social Club, or in the middle of the night—he would close his eyes and conjure up his mother's words as Birdy had whispered them to him. *Mi dulce niño. Todo va a estar bien.* My sweet boy. All will be well.

After a while, the sound of his mother's voice became the sound of Birdy's voice, and he didn't know the difference.

Sometimes Pablo got up early and went down to the shore alone, riding his bike to the boardwalk and then dropping onto the sand. At first he thought that he would take the basket off, since there was no Birdy to ride in it, but after a while he began to use it for other things. Coconuts. Sea glass. Pretty rocks that he could paint with pictures of birds, flying birds, and sell in the souvenir shop. He was branching out.

He stood at the edge of the water, tiny waves lapping over his toes, and looked out at the horizon. It was usually calm, with the breeze blowing onshore as always, lifting his hair off his neck and forehead. No winds of change had come before or after that one night, the night that Birdy flew away.

The winds of change mean fortune lost or fortune gained.

Pablo considered that old saying. It wasn't always easy to tell what was lost and what was gained. He had lost Birdy, her presence by his side. But she would have lost her freedom, maybe her life, if she hadn't soared away on the winds of change. And that would have been the worst thing he could imagine, Birdy locked up in a cage. So, in a way, hadn't he both lost and gained when she flew away?

If Birdy had been there, he would have talked to her about it. She would have listened. He missed those days. Sometimes, after making sure he was alone on the sand, Pablo spoke aloud to Birdy. Not often, but once in a while.

"I miss you, Birdy-bird," he would say. "I hope the winds are strong and the sky is clear, wherever you are."

She was a Seafarer, after all. Wherever she was, out there over the enormous ocean, she was listening.

ACKNOWLEDGMENTS

This novel gathered itself together, over years, from different sources of inspiration. I thank Alec Wilkinson of the *New Yorker* for "A Voice from the Past," his fascinating article on the properties and preservation of sound. Thanks to Steve Snyder and Nancy Forrester of Key West, whose secret garden of rescue parrots inspired the Committee. Deep thanks to my many immigrant students over the years, from whom I have learned so much. My gratitude to Diane Evia-Lanevi, Mia Munoz Garcia, Aria, Moe and Kamu Dominguez, Art Klossner and Mobius Meadows

Farm, and Ann Ramaley Garry, for their help with many details. Thanks also to Kathi Appelt, Marion Dane Bauer, and Holly McGhee for their generosity in reading a very early draft. I am grateful to my adoption group friends for their laughter and insight and support. Heather Alexander's devotion, hilarity, and enthusiasm were invaluable to me from the get-go. Ana Juan's magnificent artwork took my breath away when I saw it, and I am honored that she chose to illustrate this book. My gratitude to the extraordinary book designer Sonia Chaghatzbanian, who continues to work her magic on my books. Jeannie Ng, copy-editor extraordinaire, I so appreciate your eagle eye. I'm grateful to the lovely Sara Crowe for her grace, enthusiasm, and smarts. My thanks to Louisa Solomon and Jim Schnobrich for their patience, skill, and dedication with the audio edition of this book. My love and thanks to Mark Garry, who listened so patiently to the ideas and vision of this book the very first night I met him, and who has kept listening patiently over the years it took to write it. Finally, thank you to Caitlyn Dlouhy, who knows how to coax the spark in this book and others into flame, and who does so with such grace and insight. How lucky I am to work with her.